Syndicate Gun

Center Point
Large Print

Also by D. B. Newton and available from
Center Point Large Print:

The Savage Hills
Bounty on Bannister
Bullets on the Wind

Syndicate Gun

A Jim Bannister Western

D. B. Newton

CENTER POINT LARGE PRINT
THORNDIKE, MAINE

This Center Point Large Print edition
is published in the year 2021 by arrangement with
Golden West Literary Agency.

Originally published in the US by Berkley Medallion.

The text of this Large Print edition is unabridged.
In other aspects, this book may vary
from the original edition.
Printed in the United States of America
on permanent paper.
Set in 16-point Times New Roman type.

ISBN: 978-1-64358-849-0 (hardcover)
ISBN: 978-1-64358-853-7 (paperback)

The Library of Congress has cataloged this record under
Library of Congress Control Number: 2020950549

Syndicate Gun

CHAPTER I

The Morgantown coach, a scarred and battered mud wagon, came down off the high pass at reckless speed with brake shoes smoking, and the four team-horses scrambling in the traces. This was simply its normal way of arriving; but when it hit the floor of the gulch and boiled to a halt before the stage line office it had its only passenger, a man named Boyd Selden, white and trembling at the knees. Stepping out on solid ground Selden mopped a handkerchief over his smooth-shaven cheeks, and his hand shook. Afterward he slapped dust from well cut but rumpled clothing, while a trained glance shrewdly appraised his surroundings.

One look told the story. This had been a pro-ducing camp once, but the mine workings that scarred the walls of the gulch were abandoned now and a number of empty buildings, already decaying, showed how Morgantown had fallen into decline. Today, it was clear that such life as the place could boast depended on a few cattle outfits that had moved in and taken over the valley below, after the mines played out.

Boyd Selden hunted up the station agent;

having arranged about his luggage, he inquired next as to local law and was directed to the jail—a squat log building standing some distance farther along the twisting street. It was a pleasant day, warm here in the bottom of the gulch, with cumulus clouds in ranks sailing across a pale and windy sky of spring, and the door of the jail stood open. Selden walked inside the office to find a man with thinning hair and an untrimmed gray mustache seated behind the desk, scraping out the bowl of a pipe with a knife blade.

A nickeled badge sagged against the front of the man's unbuttoned vest. Selden nodded to his greeting and asked, "Just what are you? Sheriff, or town marshal, or what?"

"Happens I'm both marshal and sheriff's deputy for this end of the county," the other said. "The two jobs go together. Anything I can do for you—in either capacity? Sam White's the name."

"Selden. Boyd Selden."

He was sure he saw the old man's eyes flicker briefly; the hands working with knife and pipe bowl paused for the barest fraction of time. But if he had heard the name before, the lawman didn't say so. Sam White merely nodded again and pointed with the knife, saying, "Haul up a chair, Mr. Selden."

"Thank you."

While fetching it from where it stood against the wall, Selden gave the office a quick inspection—battered desk and chairs, iron stove, file case and cabinet, a cot in one corner, bulletin board with reward dodgers pinned to it. A door opened onto the cellblock at the rear. Satisfied that they were alone, he seated himself, seeing to the crease of his trousers, and laid his neat Homburg on a corner of the desk. He said, "I'd like some information about a man named Jim Bannister . . ."

This time the reaction was definite. The deputy sheriff's head jerked slightly and he dropped both hands on the desk, as sharp black eyes met the full thrust of Selden's probing stare. "Bannister?" he repeated.

"I think you know the name." A hint of cruel humor found its way into Selden's crisp voice. "I imagine it's an embarrassing one for you. As I understand it, he spent the whole of this past winter in your town—right here in this office, actually sitting in for you in the marshal's job while you were in bed with pneumonia and a bullet wound and a few other things. It wasn't until the snows melted and the passes opened and he had left, that people found out your assistant had been a wanted man himself—an outlaw with a twelve-thousand-dollar bounty on his head!"

There was a heavy stillness through which the sounds of the village came plainly—a wagon rattling past in the street, a dog barking, someone working up firewood with measured strokes of an ax. Sam White broke gaze. Deliberately, he snapped the blade of his knife shut, and dropped it and the pipe into separate pockets of his vest. Raising his eyes again he looked directly at his visitor, then said gruffly, "Don't see how I can deny what appears to be common knowledge."

Selden nodded. "At least," he commented, "you still seem to be keeping your job. Even after such a mistake in judgment . . ."

"Wouldn't that sort of be between me and my constituents?" the other retorted. "Just what do you want with me, mister?"

"With you, nothing. But this fellow Bannister and I have business. If I can, I'd like to get in touch with him."

With pointed sarcasm: "You think maybe he left a forwarding address?"

"That's exactly what I'm gambling on—it's why I've come two days out of my way. I'm a busy man," Boyd Selden said in brusque tones. "It happens I'm an official of the Western Development Corporation, out of Chicago. I should be in Silver Hill right now, on important company business."

Sam White's face was strictly unreadable. "You want me to say I was in Bannister's confidence—that I keep in touch with him even now? Would I be apt to admit it to a stranger? Above all, would I tell a Western Development man? Hell! He's wanted for killing one of your own field agents.

You're the very people who've put a twelve-thousand-dollar reward on him, for murder!"

Boyd Selden leaned forward. "If Bannister did confide in you," he said, his eyes on the other's face, "perhaps you know that he and I have already met. The man sought me out one day about a year ago to try and get my help in reopening his case and having that New Mexico conviction set aside. That took a great deal of nerve; but then, I'm willing to admit he impressed me as being no ordinary outlaw! Now it happens I'd like to talk to him again—but unless you can somehow help me get word to him, I'm smart enough to know I haven't a chance in the world of doing it."

The old lawman looked at him without any change of expression, though the fingers of one rope-scarred hand had begun to drum the desk top. Abruptly Sam White kicked back his chair and stood.

"Wait here," he grunted.

He limped slightly as he crossed the room, snagged a wide-brimmed hat off a peg beside the door and walked out, with no more explanation than that. But Boyd Selden, watching him go, wore the look of a man who felt satisfied now of getting what he wanted.

Sam White climbed the twisting street, thin sunlight warm on his shoulders and the pull of muscles in his bullet-mended leg hurting only

11

a little. Someone hailed him from the door of Irwin's barbershop, but he was engrossed in his own thoughts and went by without hearing or answering. Near the upward end of the gulch— beginning, now, to feel that leg quite a bit—he turned in at the Lloyd Canby store.

There were no customers. A brown-haired woman of thirty, as tall as the deputy himself, was arranging a shipment of kerosene lamps on a shelf; he stood a moment to admire the grace and deft economy of her movements, in the striped shirtwaist and long skirt that together set off the attractive curves of bosom and waist. Then, as Sam came farther into the room, letting the screen door close against his heel, she heard and looked about, with a quick smile of greeting. "Hello, Sam. How's the leg this morning?"

Stella Harbord had nursed and waited hand and foot on Sam White, while he fought his long winter bout with the combination of bullet wound and lung fever that had laid him low; there could never be anything but the deepest respect and the warmest regard between them. Sam nodded and, fibbing only a little, answered: "The leg's just fine. . . . I think maybe it would be a good idea if you was to step over to the office with me for a minute."

She saw his seriousness, and at once her own brown eyes sobered; she looked suddenly like a person who waits constantly for a dreaded blow to fall. "It's about Jim! You've heard bad news. . . ."

"Not *bad* news," he said hastily. "At least, it don't hardly seem like it. But I do need your advice."

When he had explained briefly, she nodded and reached for a shawl to slip about her shoulders. "Wait while I tell Mr. Canby I'm going . . ."

They found the stranger seated as Sam had left him, legs comfortably crossed, working with a nail file which he quickly pocketed as he got to his feet. His shrewd eyes showed interest in the woman's good looks, during Sam White's brief introduction: "This here's Mr. Selden. Stella Harbord. Her husband got himself killed a few months back. . . . No, you go ahead and set. Stella can have my chair." Ushering her to it while the visitor reseated himself, the lawman took up a perch on a corner of the desk. "Well?" he demanded. "What do you think, girl?"

"I'm just not sure . . ." Thoughtfully she regarded the stranger. "I suppose you have identification?"

Shrugging, he brought out a flat billfold. "There's this," he said, removing a card and placing it before her. "And this . . . And how about my club membership?"

Stella looked soberly at the various items, nodded and pushed them back to him. "I'm sorry,

13

Mr. Selden. But we're talking about a man who's fighting for his life. There are bounty hunters who'd use any kind of trickery to collect the price you people have put on Jim Bannister." Her eyes darkened angrily. "Twelve thousand dollars! It's inhuman!"

Boyd Selden had colored faintly. "Not my personal doing, Mrs. Harbord, though I can understand why it was done. Bannister killed one of our field representatives. A jury found him guilty of murder and sentenced him to hang—and then he escaped. If the reward seems out of line to you, you must remember that a company like ours finds itself in a peculiar position."

"What you mean," Sam White put in dryly, "is that you're in the position of being hated by everybody. You come out here from Chicago with all the money in the world, and you buy up good land and you squeeze the lifeblood out of people—and naturally you make a lot of enemies. Everybody knows your man, McGraw, used a couple of tough gunslingers to take Jim's horse ranch when he wouldn't sell out. They burned his place down around him, and they killed his wife—"

"That was an accident!"

The old deputy wagged his head. "It's those little accidents that help make your company so goddamned popular! Hell, it's plain enough that's the reason the syndicate's determined to have Jim

Bannister's hide, at any cost—as an object lesson for the rest of us!"

Boyd Selden scooped his identification cards from the desk, dropped them in a side pocket. "It's very evident," he said stiffly, "I've come to the wrong place. You're both friends of this outlaw's and you won't hear a word I say. I won't waste any more of your time!"

"No—wait! Please!" Stella Harbord spoke quickly, raising one hand toward him. "We're not being fair. At least you have a right to be heard. . . ."

The man looked at her in surprise and with a new respect. "Why, I thank you for that, Mrs. Harbord. I'd about given up hope of discussing this reasonably."

Sam White shrugged and said gruffly, "Let's discuss it then. Just what do you think you want with Bannister?"

"I have some information to give him."

"That so?" The deputy peered at the other from below the tangle of his brows. "All right— whatever it is that's so important, give it to Stella. If it seems worth passing on, could be she can think of a way."

"I'm sorry, but this isn't information I'd want to have fall into just anyone's hands." Selden shook his head. "I must insist that I talk to the man myself."

The lawman made an exasperated sound, but

Stella Harbord had been studying the stranger carefully and now she said, "I think you told Sam you're going on to Silver Hill. How long do you expect to be there?"

"That depends on how my business develops. It could be only a few days, or it might be a week or two."

"You'll stay at the hotel, I suppose? Would you happen to know the room number?"

"I believe it's mentioned in this letter confirming my reservation." Selden fished the letter from his pocket. She read it briefly, handed it back.

"I'll tell you the truth, Mr. Selden. I have no idea where Jim Bannister is, but I do know a place I can write to, where he should be able to get my letter. And it isn't too awfully far from Silver Hill. I'll tell him what you've told us and let him decide. If he wants to see you, I'm sure he'll find a way to do it."

Selden studied her a long minute, and finally nodded. "Fair enough," he said, taking his hat from the desk as he came to his feet. "If you'll be good enough to do that. I'll be leaving on tomorrow morning's stage; I thank you for your trouble." He offered his hand, and after a moment she gave him her own—firm and competent, he noticed, like the level regard of her clear eyes; that such a woman concerned herself with this Jim Bannister was a fact worth thinking about.

He turned to Sam White then, but the lawman appeared not to notice the outstretched hand and Selden let it fall, as he met the deputy's cold stare. With a tartness in his voice, the old man said, "If you want cards on the table, then here's mine: I come to know Jim Bannister pretty damned good, last winter, and even though he did kill that Wells McGraw jigger, I'll stand on my opinion that he's no more a murderer than I am! He's a good man that's been wronged and hounded, for a thing that was no way his fault.

"And I'll tell you right now, if I should ever hear this was some kind of a trick—then I'm gonna be tempted to go out and kill me a syndicate agent, my own self. I reckon you have my meaning!"

Boyd Selden said, coolly enough, "Your meaning would be hard to misunderstand." He nodded again to the widow, and drew on his hat as he walked out of the office.

CHAPTER II

This place called Silver Hill sprawled across a tilted flat set high in the spine of the Central Rockies. The peaks and ridges piled around it and lifted into air that was so thin a lowlander like Boyd Selden found himself reaching for enough to fill his lungs. Even in June, it was chilly here at midday.

If Morgantown had been a mining camp in decay, this one was riding a boom. Sawmills whined, freight rigs rumbled through the teeming streets where blowdown shacks and other, more substantial buildings were jumbled helter-skelter. Here and there, set apart from the general clutter, Selden even noticed a few houses that came almost near the status of mansions.

For money was being made here. It could be sensed in the constant throb of stamp mills, in the choking drift of fumes from smelters on the pine flats below town, or the rumble of a dynamite blast in one of the mine shafts honeycombing the barren ridges, that could come at any hour of day or night to shake the ground under a man's feet and set the chandeliers to chiming in the town's fancier saloons and parlor houses. As long

18

as federal statute maintained its favorable ratio to gold, silver would flow in bright streams from such camps as this; and it was Boyd Selden's mission to see his corporation had a share.

It meant pitting his wits against other men, but this was where Boyd Selden shone: It was the shifting interplay of wills, the testing of another man's quality across a polished desk, that made the zest of the game. Certainly, in three days here he had scarcely once thought about the man called Jim Bannister. . . .

He climbed the stairs to his room in the hotel, fumbled at the lock with his key—it was dark in the corridor, though it was close to high noon, for low-bellying storm clouds darkened the day and charged the air with the oppressive burden of a coming storm. His room, too, was dark, and at first he didn't see the man who sat by the window, silhouetted against the black-hung square of sky framed by the window, a gun in his lap pointed at the door.

Jim Bannister said gruffly, "Come inside and close that thing."

Numbed by surprise, Selden moved automatically and without taking his eyes from his visitor as he slowly pushed the door to until the latch clicked, and reinserted the key.

"Lock it."

He did so, still not saying anything, and afterward advanced into the room—a reasonably

19

well-equipped one for the time and place, with a good carpet on the floor and furniture that had been hauled in by mule team across the high passes. Selden dropped his Homburg onto the bed and looked at his caller, noting the stains of travel on his clothing, the dusty hat that lay on the floor next to a scuffed boot, the rifle that leaned against the window casing. He frowned at the six-shooter and asked, in what he hoped was a casual tone, "Do we need that?"

Bannister looked at the gun, almost as though he had forgotten it, and with a shrug shoved it into his holster as he came to his feet. He loomed above Boyd Selden—he was a tall fellow, and solidly built, with pale eyes and a mop of yellow hair that looked as though it could use the scissors. But his sun-darkened jaws were closely shaven, and considering that he lived the life of a wanted criminal, his Levi's and woolen shirt and denim jacket appeared clean enough. He said, "I was beginning to wonder if you'd show up. Well, it's been a comfortable place to wait."

"How did you get in?" Selden asked, and saw his nod that indicated the open window. A narrow gallery ran around all four sides of the hotel's second story; the syndicate man remembered an outside stairway that would give access from the ground.

Selden turned to a dresser where a quart bottle and glasses stood ready. He pried the cork

20

and poured drinks for them both; as he handed Bannister his, the dimness of the room was suddenly lit by a wild glare, and on the heels of the lightning the boiling clouds outside the window seemed to split wide open, directly above their heads. Startled by the clap of thunder, Selden swore; he would never grow used to the suddenness of these mountain storms.

In the next instant the rain came down with a smash; through the window, as the two stood drinking, they could hear sudden frantic activity in the street below—people yelling and scurrying for cover, a horse drumming past, hard ridden. Buildings across the street were instantly invisible behind a watery curtain that was lighted by the fitful play of lightning. Thunder crashed and collided with its own echoes reverberating among the peaks.

"A good time to be dry," Boyd Selden observed. "Have you got a horse tied out in that somewhere?"

"I put him in the hotel shed," Bannister said absently as he watched the mountain storm rake Silver Hill. Sipping his own drink, the syndicate man had a chance for a good look at that other face. He frowned at what he saw.

He thought he had never seen a man change so rapidly. In something less than a year since their previous meeting, Bannister looked somehow older, leaner, harder; deeper lines at the corners of his mouth told of the hardships and the strain of a fugitive's existence. That other time, he had still looked pretty much like what he claimed to be—an ordinary horse rancher, forced into an outlaw's role. Today, however, you could see he was being molded and honed by circumstance into an instrument too much like the ugly-looking six-shooter strapped to his leg. And for just a moment Boyd Selden felt a pang of guilt, being a part of the organization that had brought about this change.

The nearly constant cannonading of thunder drowned out his voice when he suggested a second drink. On his repeating the question, Bannister shook his head; Selden returned both glasses where he had got them, and then indicated the chair his visitor had left. "We might as well get down to business." He drew up an armchair for himself. Seated, the two men regarded one another with cautious interest while lightning flickered, and rain beat upon the gallery outside the window.

"This was your idea," Bannister pointed out.

Selden nodded. "True enough. I'll make it brief; I've done what I promised, that time last summer when you hunted me out and we had our talk. You talked well enough then, that I went back to Chicago and checked the company files to see what I could find on that man you killed. I remembered you suggested there might be

22

something in his background—evidence he was the kind of man you always claimed, that could have brought hired gunmen to force you off that New Mexico horse ranch and kill your wife. . . ."

The tall man was watching him without expression. "So what did you find?"

Slowly Selden shook his head. "Nothing. And I mean nothing at all. Except for a few payroll vouchers—routine things of the sort—Wells McGraw might never have existed, as far as the company is concerned."

It seemed to take Bannister a moment to digest this. "I don't understand! Shouldn't there be forms of some kind? Correspondence? *Somebody* was responsible for hiring this man."

"What I'm very much afraid," Boyd Selden said, "is that someone must have been through the files ahead of me, and deliberately cleaned out McGraw's records."

The other's eyes seemed almost to darken, as it hit him. "Protecting himself!" Bannister exclaimed. "There must be someone in Chicago who *knows* I'm telling the truth—and he's covering his own tracks, against the chance of its being pinned onto him!"

Boyd Selden looked at the knuckles of one hand, and nodded. "I not only suspect you're right, but I think I know who it might have been. I only wish I could prove it." He added, "Perhaps you can see now why I couldn't put any of this in a letter, or tell it to anyone else but you directly—I will not wash the company's dirty linen in public! Still, I thought you had a right to know what I found—even if it was only a blind alley."

"Maybe not quite. If *you're* beginning to believe me."

"What I might believe means nothing," Selden pointed out, "without some kind of proof that will convince my colleagues the case should be reopened. However, I'll tell you what I'm doing—quietly, and on my own. I've put the Pinkertons to work, to try their hand at finding whatever they can about McGraw."

Bannister said quickly, "I'm certain he was mixed up in something in the Dakotas. . . ."

"Then it must have been under another name. So far they've been unable to trace him to Dakota. They've followed the trail back as far as Houston, but there it stops."

"What was he doing in Houston?"

"It isn't too clear. Living from hand to mouth, apparently. That was five years ago. He had a woman there, but she seems to have vanished—the agency is checking that angle now. But for the time being there's really nothing to go on."

"I see . . ." Bannister's face was bleak. After a moment he added, "All the same, I guess I have to thank you. You're under no obligation to do anything for me."

"I'll be frank with you. I have my own enemies inside the corporation—as I think I've hinted. It would be to my advantage if I could pin Wells McGraw on the particular one I have in mind. So, I'm not being entirely disinterested."

Jim Bannister considered that, and shrugged. "All right." As though suddenly restless and unable to remain still, the big man slapped both hands flat upon his knees and swung erect, to take a pace or two about the carpet. Without their noticing, the brief storm had already blown away in a final, distant muttering of thunder. The rain had stopped and the day was growing lighter again, with a busy dripping now from the gallery eaves.

Still seated, watching the other man, Selden asked, "What do you plan to do?"

"Do?" Bannister returned his look for a moment, as though the question failed to make sense to him. "Why, the same as I've been doing: Try to keep myself alive. That's about as far as my planning goes!" He ran the palm of a hand down over his mouth and jaw, and his face looked that of a very tired and discouraged man.

Selden had no comment.

"I imagine," Bannister went on, as though thinking aloud to himself, "I'd better be thinking now about getting out of Colorado. Up to now I've hung around mostly on the chance of hearing from you. But I'm crowding my luck to stay much longer; the noose is drawing pretty tight." He turned and picked his hat from the floor and drew it on, got his rifle from where it had leaned, handy, against the window frame. "I thank you," he said again, solemnly. "If by any chance something more should turn up—you know now how to get in touch with me."

"The woman in Morgantown . . ." Boyd Selden nodded as he got up from his own chair. He saw Bannister's glance move to the open window and said, on an impulse, "You don't have to leave that way! No need crawling through windows. I'll walk down with you." At the door, hand on knob, he looked back and saw the big man standing hesitant and motionless. "Oh, good Lord!" he exclaimed. "Do you think that anyone seeing us together would believe for a minute that you could be Bannister? When they all know I'm an officer in the company that wants to see you hang?"

Bannister considered that, and a slow grin broke across his face and made it seem instantly younger and ironed some of the bitterness from it. "Don't hardly seem likely," he admitted. "All right. I'd rather use the door, any time. . . ."

The dark hall was empty. They went the length of it, Bannister carrying his rifle beneath his arm, and through a door at the end which opened onto the gallery. The clouds were breaking and the sun was out, a blinding dazzle; the life of the town

26

had already resumed its normal pace after being driven briefly indoors by the hammering storm. When they reached the flight of wooden steps Selden went down first, sensing that Bannister would feel uncomfortable putting his back to any man.

Behind the big block of the hotel building was the horse shed where guests who owned animals could stable them. Water dripped from the eaves, spears of flashing sunlight. While Selden waited, Bannister entered and a moment afterward came out leading a lineback dun gelding, a chunky-looking animal, saddled and ready to travel, the rifle standing now in the leather scabbard. Selden fell in beside him and they walked toward the street, and at the hotel's corner stopped while Jim Bannister gave a long and searching scrutiny to the traffic along the sidewalks and the puddled, muddy thoroughfare. Apparently satisfied, he found the stirrup and swung astride. He looked down at Selden. "Well—"

There was suddenly nothing more to say. Bannister raised a hand, briefly, in a kind of half-salute. After that he reined away, into the street, and touched the dun horse with his heels and lifted it into an easy canter. Mud and rain-water gouted up beneath the dun's shod hoofs as its rider fell into the flow of traffic in the busy street.

Hands in pockets and head bare to the warm

27

sun, Selden lingered a moment to watch him go, thinking that he would likely never see this man again. When a lumbering ore wagon rolled between, the driver swearing and whipping his mules as they fought the sluggish footing, Selden turned away—already half forgetting Bannister, his businessman's brain turning to the interview he had scheduled for the coming afternoon.

It was at that instant he felt a breath of air on his cheek and heard a sound, almost like a fingernail tapping against the wooden siding of the building at his elbow. Immediately afterward came the snap of the rifle shot.

Not really believing what was happening, he jerked his head about. For just a moment he could see, against a background of sun-drenched sky and dazzling white cloud bank, the hunched shape of a man kneeling on a shed roof directly across the way. He saw him work a rifle's lever and then press the stock again to his cheek. In the cold horror of the moment Selden realized no one but himself was aware at all of his danger— that everything proceeded as usual, the traffic of wagons and horsemen flowing about him, oblivious and busy with their own affairs.

Boyd Selden started to pivot where he stood, frantically seeking cover. There was none. It could only have been a matter of seconds; then the rifle spoke again, the crack of its report carrying to him above the jumble of other sounds.

28

Boyd Selden felt a numbing blow and knew that he was hit.

Almost in slow motion he was seized and slammed, hard, against the hotel clapboards. He slipped helplessly down into the mud, and into darkness.

CHAPTER III

Over the noise of the street, Jim Bannister did not hear either shot. It was sheer chance that he happened to look back, in pulling wide of the ore wagon to avoid being drenched with muddy water spewed up by its wheels and the lunging hoofs of the mules. Thus he glimpsed Boyd Selden's odd behavior—the man's sudden panicky turn, the jerky movements that struck him as those of a man confronted by terror and not knowing how to escape.

When the lumbering rig cut off his view, Bannister was enough concerned that he swore and gave the dun a kick. To get another view of the syndicate man, he had to swing around the rear end of the wagon; when he did Selden was already falling, thrown hard by the force of a bullet.

It never occurred to Bannister but what the man was dead; there had been the disjointed, jerky collapse of death in the way he fell, like a puppet flung aside. The assassin had had a perfect target and all the time he needed, apparently, to take at least two shots—even yet, no one else in the busy street seemed aware of what had happened.

Bannister himself might have sat stunned by the suddenness of the thing, except that months on the dodge had honed his reflexes to a fine edge. Almost without thought he sent his horse again into motion.

Though he assumed he could do nothing for the victim, there remained the one who had shot him. He remembered Selden appeared to have been staring toward the street's far side, in the seconds before he was struck down. Bannister reined that way, so sharply that the dun missed its footing and both man and horse nearly went down into the slop.

A hard jerk at the leathers helped straighten the animal out; he cut sharply across the path of a couple of horsemen, who cursed him, and drawing his belt gun jumped the gutter that swirled with rust-brown runoff of the storm.

The shots might have come from any of the doors or windows facing the hotel, but directly opposite the spot where Boyd Selden went down Bannister spotted a slant-roofed shed, shouldering between its larger neighbors. On an impulse he sent the dun past this and as he broke into the alley beyond was rewarded by sight of a figure sprinting away from him, the skirts of an unfastened yellow slicker flapping, a rifle clamped beneath one arm.

Bannister went after him.

The drum of hoofs coming up behind him gave

31

the fellow warning; in mid-stride he stopped and whirled, raising the rifle. He quickly changed his mind and plunged on without using it, but not before giving the other a glimpse of untrimmed sandy whiskers and protruding eyes in a sallow face. Bannister yelled at him to halt, only to see him change course and dart for cover behind the nearest building corner.

Bannister could have fired but he saved the bullet, using his spurs instead. Drumming after the fugitive, he was too furious to consider he might be met by a head-on blast from the rifle; as it happened, he found himself confronted only by a high board fence. Pulling up, he stood in the stirrups to look across into a lumber yard— orderly piles of clean yellow boards, dark from the recent rain, and putting out a heady sweetness of pine smell.

Though there was no sign of the other man, he could only have scaled the fence. It was much too high for the dun to follow. Bannister simply bellied across it from the saddle, dropping to a crouch amid sawdust and woodchips that littered the ground beyond.

Listening and hearing nothing, he rose and moved on with gun ready to the closest of the stacks and eased around it; and now he was surrounded by the piles of wood, ranging away in orderly rows. Searching, he caught a flick of shadow crossing a corridor up ahead, and threw a shot at it. He missed, and knew it, and started forward—to duck for cover an instant later, as a rifle opened up with a flash of fire and the angry thwack of a bullet striking lumber just beside his head.

Blocked from that direction, Jim Bannister spun and made for the far end of the lumber pile and then forward, along a parallel corridor that should bring him up behind the man with the rifle. The noontime stillness was complete, the racks of wood seeming to have sopped up the gun sound like blotting paper. Bannister kept his breathing shallow and let the sawdust chips muffle the sound of his boots, though it was impossible to quiet entirely the occasional chime of a spur rowel. He tested each open space between the rows before he ventured across it, and slowed to a cautious prowl as he judged he was nearing the place where the one with the rifle might still be holed up, waiting.

There was no trace of him. There was nothing at all until, in his cautious search, Bannister's boot toe touched a bright bit of metal and, stooping, he picked up the casing from a new rifle shell. It still held a faint swirl of smoke, and this was where the fugitive had stood as he levered a fresh cartridge into the breech. The man himself was gone, making his escape out the forward end of the lumberyard, past the sheds and the steam sawmill that was closed down and silent at the noon hour. He would be lost, by this time, in the crowded streets and huddled buildings of the busy silver camp.

Jim Bannister flung aside the empty shell and, having replaced the load in his own revolver, put it away and reluctantly retraced his course through the lumber stacks and climbed the fence again. The dun waited patiently where he'd left it; he dropped into leather and sent the horse back along the alley, concerned now to learn how it was with Boyd Selden.

He found some half-dozen people had stopped to look at the syndicate man lying where the sniper's bullets had spilled him. They were doing nothing, merely staring; and Bannister, lighting down, ordered them aside. Boyd Selden was not dead—he lay on his back, with one leg bent under him and his eyes glazed with shock, but he was breathing shallowly. Ignoring the curious questions that were thrown at him, Bannister went to one knee beside the hurt man.

He saw the blood then. Selden had been struck high in the left shoulder, and the bullet shock had knocked him out. As Bannister ripped open the shirt for a closer look, a woman's voice said, "Is he bad hurt?"

He had had enough of questions and answered shortly, without looking around, "He could use a doctor, if anybody in this crowd had the wits to fetch one!"

34

"Wouldn't it be better if we took him to the doctor instead?"

The suggestion made him turn his head in some surprise. While he was occupied with Boyd Selden a handsome carriage, all polished metal-work and gleaming black leather and shining yellow wheels, had pulled up at the curb. A liveried black man held the reins; the woman who sat alone, holding an opened parasol, looked too well dressed for a raw mining town like Silver Hill. She told her driver, "Get down, George, and lend a hand getting him into the carriage."

As the black man wrapped his reins about the whipstock, Jim Bannister said quickly, "There's considerable blood. I won't guarantee against messing the upholstery."

"It's leather. It can be cleaned." She did not seem too much concerned, and Bannister was not going to argue this unexpected offer of help— only a doctor could say how bad that shoulder wound might be. Selden was already stirring a little; when with the driver's help Bannister got him onto his feet, he was actually able to stagger a few steps as they half carried him between them toward the waiting carriage, while the curious crowd stood watching. The woman had moved over to make room on the leather seat. It was a job, but they lifted Selden in and Bannister followed, after tying his horse on behind.

When the carriage gave with a lurch to the

weight of the driver taking his seat, Selden mumbled and opened his eyes. Bannister had to place a hand on his uninjured shoulder to steady him. "Easy! You've been shot!"

The colored driver got his horses into motion, and without regard for traffic made a wide U-turn that nearly cramped the carriage wheels. Selden was thrown off balance and a groan tore from him; Bannister caught and held him upright. The black man got his team straightened out and sent them back along the street into the center of town.

Selden appeared badly dazed, his face drained and gray. Jim Bannister wasn't at all sure the man understood as he explained: "Someone used a rifle on you, from across the street. I don't know how bad the damage is. But the lady here was good enough to offer us a lift to the doctor's."

The man only blinked at him, and then turned his attention to the person seated on the other side of him, "Mrs. Gentry!" he mumbled.

"That's me," she said, nodding. "And you're the man from the syndicate—we met in J. T.'s office." She added, "I was just out for a little spin, after the storm. Glad to be useful . . ."

Bannister gave her a closer look. She was still young, probably under thirty, and attractive enough—full-blown, with the round cheeks and complexion of a bisque doll. Her hair, of a good sorrel color, was curled and frizzed in what he supposed must be the latest fashion; the color of her cheeks and mouth was obviously too high to be natural—in that puritanical age, something to be looked on as not quite respectable. She smelled of face powder and toilet water.

The carriage, and the full-skirted green outfit with jacket and feathered bonnet to match, indicated that someone was spending considerable money on her, yet there was obviously very common clay in her—which made little difference in Jim Bannister's eyes. She seemed friendly, and putting herself out in this way to help a wounded man showed she had a heart and consideration for others. He had to respect those qualities, wherever he met them.

Boyd Selden shifted position and sucked in a breath at the pain of his arm. Bannister said quickly, "Careful with that, till we know how bad it's damaged. I have hopes the bullet never struck bone, but the doctor will have to tell us. . . ."

They had not very far to go. The building was a small one, crowded in among other, more substantial structures; the board nailed above the door carried the name of Jonah Staples, M. D. The carriage rocked to a halt and again the black driver got down to help Bannister with the hurt man. When they reached the door the woman was already there to hold it open for them.

The waiting room was deserted. As they got Selden inside, the doctor himself came through

37

another door, a slight man with gray mutton-chops, wearing a set of pince-nez on a black string. He was buttoning a shirt-sleeve, but one glance at the injured syndicate man set him rolling it up again. "In here," he said brusquely.

Selden, his knees like rubber, let himself be maneuvered into a smaller room that contained a cabinet of instruments and a makeshift operating table. They put him on a chair and the doctor looked over his head at Bannister, who tapped his own left shoulder and said, "Rifle bullet."

In the doorway the woman said, "Treat him good, Doc. J. T. wouldn't want it thought Silver Hill ain't safe for people that come here to do honest business."

The doctor nodded brusquely. "Sure thing, Flora. All you folks clear out and leave me with him." He measured Bannister's big frame with a glance and added, "Maybe you better stick close—in case I need a hand holding him down."

Bannister nodded, and followed the woman and her driver out into the empty waiting room; the doctor closed the door after them.

Flora Gentry told her driver, "Go on out to the carriage." Alone, she turned to face Jim Bannister. She was not a tall woman and had to tilt her head back and to one side in order to look up at him, past the sweep of the feather on her hat brim. She had brought her parasol and tapped it nervously against the toe of one high-topped, pointed shoe, while a frown troubled her smooth and full-cheeked face. "Just what *did* happen to him, mister?"

"You've heard all I know," Bannister told her. "Maybe Boyd Selden will have an idea who was holding the rifle, when there's a chance to ask."

"Did you get a look at him?"

"Only a glimpse."

She twirled her parasol to the right and then to the left, while brown eyes held upon his face. He thought there was a shrewd intelligence in them. Finally the woman nodded. "I'd say it's a job for the constable. If I can find him, I'll send him over to talk to you."

She was gone, with a swirl of skirts, leaving the scent of perfume and face powder. Jim Bannister felt the quick alarm that tightened his cheek muscles.

Constable! By this time he had thought surely to be gone from Silver Hill; instead he found himself getting involved in something he wanted no part of, especially if it meant facing the local law. He looked toward the door. Flora Gentry's carriage was just pulling away, but he could see his horse standing at the iron hitch-post where the driver had tied it. His impulse was to walk out and get into the saddle and ride from here, while there was time.

But he couldn't do that, for his obligation to Boyd Selden held him. Selden, even if for his own selfish reasons, had taken the trouble to check his story and set the Pinkertons to work on it. Now someone in this town had tried to murder Boyd Selden and might try again. Jim Bannister felt a strong responsibility.

He was still there—seated on one of the chairs in the waiting room, his hat on the table beside him while he stolidly smoked down a cigarette— when the inner door opened. Dr. Staples said, "Your friend didn't know if you'd still be here or not, but he wants to talk to you."

Jim Bannister nodded and, stubbing out his cigarette, picked up his hat and followed the man into the other room.

CHAPTER IV

Boyd Selden, with shirt and coat lying in a heap on the floor by his chair, was having a stiff drink from a tumbler the doctor had filled for him; his hand shook slightly and his face was almost as white as the bandage on his shoulder. "I feel like a fool," he said, "laid out by a mere flesh wound. But—I've never been shot before."

Bannister assured him, "Bullet shock can flatten the very toughest."

"He's lucky," the doctor commented. "Another inch and that arm would have been chewed up until I might not have saved it. Or, the bullet could just as well have killed him. As it is, he'll have a stiff shoulder for a month—nothing worse."

A final adjustment to the sling that held the syndicate man's hurt arm immobilized, and Staples turned away and took a coat from its hook on the wall. "While you finish your drink, I'll get ahold of my kid and send him to the hotel for those things you want. I can't have you moving around until you're sure you've got your legs under you." He waited for the injured man's nod and then went out, leaving Bannister alone with him.

Boyd Selden took a swallow of the whiskey and shuddered. Sharp eyes, bright with pain, searched Bannister's. "Now maybe you can tell me what happened!"

Bannister frowned. "I'd have thought you were in the best position to do that. When I left you by the corner of the hotel, I just happened to look back and saw you behaving as though you were terrified and trying to escape from something. A second later you went down and I knew you'd been shot, but the one that did it got away from me. Then that woman offered to help—whoever she was."

"Flora Gentry," the syndicate man supplied, and smiled faintly. "Quite a female, isn't she? She's J. T. Herron's mistress."

"And who's J. T. Herron?"

Selden gave him a look. "You hadn't heard of him? He's the big wheel in this camp, the man I'm chiefly here to deal with: a roughneck who came from the East somewhere and made a fortune in silver—and a legend of himself, here in Colorado. He owns half a dozen producing properties in Silver Hill, along with the hotel and the bank and anything else worth having. He could buy and sell nearly any man in the state. In fact, rumor has it he actually bought Flora Gentry—paid her husband cash on the line for her: but now he can't marry her because he has a wife in Denver or somewhere who won't give him a divorce."

"The Gentry woman struck me as a decent sort of person," Bannister observed.

"Perhaps not exactly a lady," Boyd Selden said, "but I have no call to say anything against her—especially not after what she just did for me."

He drained off the rest of his drink, set the glass aside. "Right now I'm not concerned about J. T. Herron. I want to know who it was tried to kill me!"

"You didn't see him?"

"Not really. The first shot missed and I just had a glimpse of someone with a rifle, on the roof of a shed across the street—no knowing how long he may have waited for his chance at me. All I could tell was that he had on a yellow slicker. I was hoping you'd got a better look."

Bannister told of the chase and the brief gun duel in the lumberyard. "The fellow was slight-built, with sandy hair and beard. Not much to go by—except, perhaps his eyes."

"What about his eyes?"

The tall man narrowed his own, trying to call them again to mind. "One—the left—showed more white than the other. Looked to me he might have damaged it. . . ."

He knew from Selden's reaction that he had struck pay dirt. But in that moment somebody had entered the outer office and came tramping directly back. They both looked around at the man who loomed in the door of the operating room. Jim Bannister went suddenly tense, seeing the glimmer of metal pinned to an unbuttoned waistcoat.

"Your name's Selden?" The newcomer spoke without preliminary. He looked to be about fifty, too heavy, with jowls that gave a bulldog set to his face, but his black eyes had a directness and a competence as they studied the injured man. "I think I've seen you around. I'm Tom Slate— town constable. Mrs. Gentry tells me you been involved in a shooting."

"As you can see." Selden indicated his bandaged arm. The black eyes regarded it, then swung to Bannister who was already preparing himself to meet the lawman's questions. But Selden got in first with his own answers: "This is Jim Bowers, Constable—in my employ."

"Oh?" Bannister endured the scrutiny, waiting for the first hint that the constable had remembered a description on a reward dodger, or a picture in a newspaper article. But with no real sign of interest, Tom Slate turned back to the syndicate man.

"So somebody in my town don't like you," he grunted. "Considering the outfit you represent, maybe that ain't too much a surprise. Guess there ain't no love lost, anywhere in this country, on that Chicago crowd!"

Boyd Selden started to bristle—like a man constantly on the defense, Bannister thought. "A shot from ambush—" he began. The constable overrode him.

"Sure, I agree, it ain't to be allowed. That's the reason I'm talking to you. Tell me anything you know that might help me tracking down the gent that used the rifle."

"As it happens," the syndicate man said, still angry, "I think I know who it was. He got away but Bowers has given me a good description. Perhaps you know a man named Ed McIver?"

The constable repeated the name, frowning. "A miner—partner with Lewt Flagg? They work a claim up on Turkey Ridge. . . ."

"That's right."

"You been having some kind of trouble with that pair? Any reason one or both of them would like to put you out of action?"

Selden denied it. "No trouble," he declared emphatically. "I did make them a business proposition. But you said it yourself—men like me are sometimes hated without any cause for it."

The constable looked again at Bannister. "Just how certain are you of your identification?"

"I'm not certain of anything," the latter said, returning his look. "I've never seen this Ed McIver, that I know of. But Selden says he fits the description of the one who got away from me after the ambushing."

Tom Slate considered this, looking thoughtfully at Bannister. Finally he reached a decision.

"Only one sure way to know. Happens I ran into McIver, not ten minutes ago. You come with me and we'll have you take a look at him."

Bannister hesitated. Selden must have read correctly the startled glance the tall man shot at him, for he said quickly, "*I'll* go. I'm the one he tried to kill." He started to his feet, and had to clutch at the table edge as weakness overcame him. The lawman shook his head, his manner firm.

"Stay where you are. You're not in any shape to go anywhere. Maybe McIver was the one tried to kill you, Selden, and maybe he wasn't. In any event Bowers is my witness, not you." The hurt man plainly had no choice; he dropped back into his chair, as Slate's probing stare lifted again to the tall stranger. "Any reason you don't *want* to come with me, mister?"

Bannister met the look. "No reason at all," he said coolly. "I'm ready when you are."

Tom Slate nodded and swung toward the door; a last exchange of glances with the frowning syndicate man, and Jim Bannister picked up his hat and, however reluctantly, followed.

With the swiftness of mountain weather, the last remains of storm clouds had melted, and the mud streets and plank walks and crowded buildings of Silver Hill were all steaming under a sparkling, sun-filled sky. Even now one felt the thinness of the air, and in the shadows the wind carried a chill edge.

The rhythmic pound of the stamps kept pace with them as Bannister and the constable made their way through the heavy, busy traffic; somewhere, exploding dynamite rumbled underground. The regular inhabitants of the town scarcely seemed aware of such things, long since grown used to them, and to the evil-odored fumes from the smelters.

Tom Slate spoke little, but led the way across the wide street and along it for a block, to an unpainted plank building that housed a restaurant of sorts. Ushered in ahead of the lawman, Bannister entered a long, low-ceilinged room, with canvas tacked to its unfinished walls and stretched overhead for a ceiling. Men crowded the length of the trestle table that filled most of the room, and the several smaller ones were likewise occupied.

Bannister, in the doorway, scanned the place without seeing a face he recognized; then Slate, coming up beside him, indicated a round table in a corner, near a large iron space heater set in a box of cinders. As they started that way, through a steaming swirl of food smells and odors of wet wool and sweating men, one of the half-dozen seated at the table glanced up and Bannister saw the narrow face, the sandy straggle of beard and the damaged left eye showing more white than its mate. The way the man returned the look, his half-finished meal suddenly forgotten, was all he

47

needed to tell him he had been remembered in turn.

Ed McIver's companions, like himself, had the rough clothing and weathered look of working miners or prospectors, and they seemed engrossed in some kind of earnest talk. The talk died as they saw the man with the star looming above them. Tom Slate said, in his carrying voice, "Do you pick him out, Mr. Bowers?"

"Yes," Bannister said. "That one."

His face grim, Slate nodded. "All right, McIver. I think you better come along."

Silence spread through the room, like ripples on a pond. The accused man seemed unable to move. It was the one seated next to him—a hulking, black-jowled fellow, with an aggressive jaw and cheeks pitted by some old disease—who found tongue to demand loudly, "What the hell is this?"

Slate looked at him. "A little charge of attempted murder, Flagg."

A dropped fork chimed against a plate. Someone echoed, *"Murder!"* And now chair legs scraped as McIver stumbled to his feet, crying harshly, "I don't know what the hell you're talking about!"

"You own a rifle?"

For an instant the man seemed about to deny it, apparently decided not to with all the eyes watching him. Instead he retorted, "What if I do?"

48

"Here's a witness who says you tried to kill a man named Boyd Selden with it."

Bannister, watching the accused man, saw that he looked ashen and badly upset. And no wonder, Jim Bannister thought suddenly. This was all a bad surprise. He'd been supposing the man he shot was dead!

Someone at the table said, "That's a serious charge, Constable!"

"It's meant to be!" Tom Slate answered without taking his eyes from the accused man. "What do you say, McIver? You going to claim you didn't know anybody named Selden?"

The one he called Flagg was on his feet now. "Of course Ed knew him! Every man here had reason to. We all got workings on Turkey Ridge, and Selden and his syndicate want them. We been holding meetings to decide how to stop them from cleaning us off and taking over the whole damn ridge!"

"If my witness is telling it straight," Tom Slate suggested dryly, "could be you decided the best way to stop it was with a rifle bullet."

Flagg's black stare settled on Jim Bannister. "You still ain't told us just who the hell your witness *is!*"

"His name is Bowers. He works for Selden. . . ."

At that, Flagg swore savagely. "A syndicate flunky! By God! I might have guessed!" His palm, striking the table top, caused the dishes to chime and jump. "Let *us* hear your story, mister. It ought to be a good one!"

"You're under no obligation to tell them anything," the constable reminded Bannister as the latter hesitated. "But since they know this much I'd like them to have it all."

The tall man shrugged. "It's soon told," he said shortly, and pointed at McIver. "I don't claim to have seen the actual shooting, but I know for certain this is the man who gave me a chase afterwards. He had a rifle and he was wearing a yellow slicker—and his description fits the one Selden got a glimpse of, just before he was shot down."

"Damn country's full of yellow slickers!" Flagg retorted loudly. "They all look exactly alike. Any fool knows that!"

Bannister would not be baited. "McIver turned and looked me in the face, when he was not much farther from me than he is right now. Later when I had him cornered he opened up on me with his rifle and he shot to kill. . . ."

The scream that broke from the accused man sounded scarcely human. It was more like the cry of a trapped and goaded animal, and the look that contorted his face was a good match for it; in a half crouch, there between the table and the wall, he made a convulsive movement and his hand appeared, clutching the hogleg revolver he had brought out from somewhere in his clothing.

Only frenzied haste could have made him miss, at that range. Bannister saw the smear of muzzle flame and smoke, took the roar of the weapon like a blow against his face, almost thought he felt the faint tap of concussion when the bullet disturbed the air in passing. Behind him there was a belated outbreak of yelling as men scurried for cover, in an overturning of chairs and jarring of tables.

And because Ed McIver was certain to try again, Jim Bannister had no choice. He whipped the gun from his own holster with a practised move that, a year ago, would have been beyond him. The weapon swept up and the hammer dropped, punching a shot into the second ear-shattering report of McIver's revolver. Hit squarely in the chest, McIver was driven back to strike the wall with head and shoulders; rebounding, his knees buckled and he dropped forward across the table, rolling from there to the floor in a clattering sweep of dirty dishes.

The exchange of bullets had caught McIver's friends wholly by surprise, staring with stunned expression into the slow drift of blue smoke. But now one slid out of his chair, to kneel beside Bannister's victim. Aghast, he lifted his head and looked around him.

Into the cottony silence left by the roar of the guns he announced in a hollow voice, "He's dead!"

51

CHAPTER V

"Murdered!" the man called Flagg corrected him in a voice that shook with fury. "Murdered by a stinking syndicate gun!"

Eyes turned to Bannister and unconsciously he let his hand tighten on the smoking revolver. But Constable Tom Slate spoke quickly. "You know better than that! McIver started shooting before the big man even touched holster. To me, it had the earmarks of a guilty conscience." He looked at one of the Turkey Ridge miners. "Murrow, what about it? You're not a man that loses his head. What do you say?"

Bannister had noticed this Murrow—a sober, little-smiling man with the heavy arms and shoulders of a toiler. He might be a shade slow in his thinking but he had the manner of someone who would pursue a thought, doggedly, until he worked it out. He said now, frowning with troubled intensity, "I just don't know what to think, Mr. Slate. Ed was a broody kind of fellow, all right. I guess maybe—if he thought he was justified—"

"Hell!" The dead man's partner was not to be silenced. "What happened just now," Lewt

Flagg declared harshly, "proves nothing more than that a man can lose his head when he's pressured! Slate, you had no case against Ed McIver and you still ain't! You ain't even told us yet when this shootin' is supposed to have happened."

The constable looked at Jim Bannister, who answered, "It was little less than an hour ago. . . ."

Flagg flung out his hands. "You see?" he told his friends. "They've murdered Ed for nothing! An hour ago we were all of us in the bar at the Colorado House—Ed McIver, too. We came directly from there." His mouth took on an ugly sneer; his stare challenged Bannister. "So, somebody has either made a damn bad mistake, or he's lying in his teeth!"

The tall man met the look, keeping a hard grip on his own temper. "Unless this man had a twin," he said quietly, "then an hour ago he was on the roof of a shed across from the hotel, waiting to ambush Boyd Selden. I stand on that!"

The issue couldn't have been clearer, and it made a bad decision for the law officer. He looked from Bannister to Flagg, and then to the other miners standing about the table. "The rest of you all in agreement with Flagg?" he asked. "McIver was with you?"

A few heads nodded and one man retorted, "You heard him, didn't you?"

Tom Slate frowned, deeply troubled. He pulled off a low-crowned hat, ran a palm across a bald spot in his grizzled hair. "Looks like an impasse," he said finally, "and the man who might have cleared it up is dead. Don't seem to leave me much to act on; but maybe the judge will have a different idea." He drew the hat on again, and peered about him uncomfortably at the roomful of stunned and silent men, and at the swinging door where the kitchen crew was peering in, aghast. "A hell of a way to have a meal interrupted!" he admitted. "I'll have this body moved as quick as possible." Turning abruptly, he halted as he looked at Bannister. "You coming?"

"Am I charged with anything?"

"Not at the moment," the constable said. "I just thought you'd want to be along while I talk to your boss. Far as this particular shooting is concerned, there's at least two dozen witnesses saw McIver start it. I only wish every killing I have to handle was as clear-cut a case of self defense!"

That had probably been said for Lewt Flagg's benefit. McIver's partner did not seem much impressed. He made an ugly sound but no one else seemed ready to argue matters—too bewildered, perhaps, by events that came too fast.

Jim Bannister suddenly realized that he still held the gun with which he had shot McIver. He slid it into the holster but kept a hand on it as he said, "I'm with you, Constable."

It was not the easiest thing he had ever done, to turn his back on that table, and the stares of hating eyes, and walk out at the lawman's side as the first babble of excited talk began behind them.

They left a room where no one now thought much of eating. Men came crowding to peer at McIver lying crumpled against the wall, the blood bright on his shirt. There seemed no inclination to move him; that was something they all seemed willing to leave for the constable.

The Turkey Ridge miners were stammering questions for which Lewt Flagg had ready answers. "The whole thing is plain enough," he told them. "Selden and his hired gun thought they could put a scare into us and make us knuckle under. They'll find out we ain't that easy to scare! It'll take more than this!" He pointed a shaking finger at the body at their feet.

Jud Murrow, the thoughtful one, had been keeping quiet while he worked at something that bothered him. Unable longer to hold it back, he got Flagg's attention and reluctantly brought it out: "Lewt, I been thinking. What we told the constable wasn't exactly right—I mean, about Ed McIver being with us during the whole past hour. Because I remember now, I didn't see him there with the rest of you when I walked in the bar."

"Of course he was there!" Flagg retorted. And when the other doggedly shook his head, the big fellow made an abrupt gesture as he conceded, "Well, maybe he went out to the can for a minute—how would I remember? Did you notice when he *did* come in?"

Murrow hesitated. "No. No, I didn't."

"There, you see? That's just the kind Ed was: A quiet fellow like that, he could be around and nobody even be aware of it. . . . But, by God, he was a hard worker and a good partner!" Lewt Flagg added, on a note of hot indignation, "It's a fine thing, when the syndicate can make him out a bushwhacker and then shoot him dead because he tries to deny it! Do it once and they can do it again—to any of us. All the more reason why we got to stand together!"

And no man in the Turkey Ridge crowd—not even Jud Murrow—appeared to question that.

Boyd Selden was evidently beginning to feel the damage to his shoulder, in spite of medication and an expert job of bandaging. His face was drawn and pale and he appeared short-tempered, as he sat in the doctor's waiting room and heard Constable Slate's report of the attempt to arrest Ed McIver. A man who is not used to being hurt, Bannister thought, is apt to make a greater fuss about it than someone who has learned by hard training to take it in his stride.

He made a sour grimace and shook his head.

"Too bad you couldn't have arrested the man, instead of pushing him in a corner. He was an excitable type—I could almost have predicted he'd break and do something wild, under pressure."

The constable said gruffly, "I take the blame for that, I was so concerned with making his friends see I had a good case, I didn't think about McIver losing his head. When he started shooting, Bowers could do no more than protect himself." He frowned. "But that don't explain the alibi the rest of them gave him."

"McIver was the man I chased into the lumber yard," Bannister insisted flatly. "What they say can't change that."

"Still, it's their word against yours—and most of those people I'd have pegged for honest men." The lawman shook his head. "Yet I have to admit, it does look as though they're lying now."

"Of course, they're lying," Selden interrupted impatiently. "I dare say they drew straws to see which would be the one to use the rifle!"

"They all do seem pretty much worked up against you," the lawman admitted, his expression solemn. "There was real hard words, about you *and* your company. They claim they're being threatened. . . ."

"Nonsense!" Boyd Selden snapped. "I won't deny that we're interested in the Ridge—our experts feel it has a good potential, in keeping

57

with the production figures from the rest of the camp. But we contend it would take our kind of capital to consolidate and develop it properly, as a unit, and not piecemeal as is now being done. Still, it's utter foolishness that we've used any threats."

Tom Slate made a dry sound in his throat. "It could be, the mere existence of an outfit the size of yours acts like a threat on some people!" Abruptly, the constable turned to the door. "I can't see there's much use pursuing this McIver shooting." He looked at Jim Bannister. "Bowers, I'm going to ask you to stay handy. I still have to talk to the judge; it's for him to decide if he wants a formal hearing. I'll be calling on you."

"He'll be here," Boyd Selden promised quickly before Bannister could reply. As though satisfied with that, Slate nodded, pulled on his hat, and left.

Alone in the waiting room, Bannister turned on the syndicate man. "Why did you tell him that? You don't expect me to let him bring me in front of a judge?"

"You still think someone will recognize you?" Selden said. "Not in this town. Forget it."

"No town's safe for me, and you know it. I've been in this one far too long already!"

But the other man shook his head. "I told you before, no one who knows me is going to suppose for a minute that the man with me could be Jim

58

Bannister—the man my company wants to hang. The constable, the judge, or anybody else—it would simply never occur to them."

"I guess that makes sense," Bannister admitted. "But I still don't like pressing my luck, to no purpose. My horse is outside. I see no reason why I shouldn't get on him and leave this place before I'm in worse trouble."

Boyd Selden considered this for a long moment, while the sounds of the camp reached into the quiet room—the busy rumble of traffic, the whine of a sawmill, the constant throb of stamps that became as much a part of a man, here, as the beat of his own pulse. Finally the syndicate man nodded. "Very well," he said. "I suppose I can cover for you with the judge, and the constable. Unless of course somebody should have better results, the next time they try something like this." And he touched his bandaged shoulder.

"You really think they will?"

"Well, you saw the temper of that Turkey Ridge crowd. They want to be rid of me."

"If I were one of them," Bannister said, "I might feel exactly the same. Remember, I fought your syndicate myself once—and lost!"

That brought quick color to the other's cheeks. He said sharply, "Don't judge me by Wells McGraw! Perhaps you had a fair grievance; these men don't. Nobody's out to rob them."

"They think otherwise."

"I've already told you," Boyd Selden snapped back at him, "It's perfectly true my company would like to gain control of Turkey Ridge, for its own purposes; but there's nothing unethical in that! Besides, the biggest obstacle isn't any of those small operators, but J. T. Herron himself. His Teakettle mine is the key. He's no mining man, after all—nothing but a promoter, a clown, with a lot of blind luck and a gift for making a profit from everything he touches. I've been sent to Silver Hill to try, once and for all, to close a deal with him."

"And once you control the Teakettle, you figure it's no real trick to get the other operators off the Ridge?" Bannister concluded.

"By legitimate means, Bannister!" the other pointed out quickly. "By fair and legitimate means! I keep telling you that. Remember it— whatever those people would try to have you believe."

"I hope it's the truth. Anyway, it's none of my concern," the tall man added, with a shrug. He took his hat from a table where he had laid it, restless to go.

He stopped as Boyd Selden said flatly, "Bannister, I'll pay you a hundred dollars a day to *make* it your concern. . . ." When the other turned a blank look on him he added, pointedly, "You can use the money, can't you?"

Bannister broke off his staring. "A man in my

position," he said, "can always use money! But, what would I have to do for it?"

"Stay until my job is finished. Make sure nothing more happens to me while I'm in Silver Hill."

"You want me for a bodyguard?"

"You could call it that."

"I'll be damned!" Suddenly Jim Bannister was laughing without much humor. And Boyd Selden's eyes hardened.

"What amuses you?"

"A few minutes ago, that McIver fellow's friends accused me of being a hired gun for the syndicate. That was funny enough! But here you are, actually suggesting it!"

"A bodyguard!" Selden retorted, anger roughening his voice. "Nothing more."

"And supposing I say I'm not interested?"

His eyes completely cold, the syndicate man answered, "It may not have occurred to you that all I have to do is mention your real name to Constable Slate. . . ."

There was a whisper of metal sliding from leather; without warning, Jim Bannister's long-barreled gun was in his hand and its muzzle rested on the man seated before him. "Has it occurred to *you,*" he suggested, quietly, "that I could kill you right now?"

He saw the other's skin turn the color of chalk, saw his chest swell to a sudden caught breath.

61

He let Selden look at the black bore of the gun long enough for his words to sink in; then, with a shake of the head, he lowered the weapon. "No, Selden," he said. "I don't think either of us really believes such things of the other. If we had, you'd never have asked me to meet you here in Silver Hill—and I would never have come!"

Selden let himself begin to breathe again as the gun returned to its holster. His color was poor and his voice held a raw tremor. "You gave me a bad moment!"

"I suppose I did," the tall man agreed. "And I guess I owe you an apology. After all, you went out of your way to try to check my story. On your own hook you've even brought in the Pinkertons to work out a backtrail on Wells McGraw."

"There's that," Selden answered. "And perhaps even more." He came to his feet, despite the weakness that made him place a hand on a chair-back for support. "Look, Bannister. I told you about having a personal enemy on the highest level of this organization, the same one, I'm convinced, who was responsible for hiring McGraw and turning him loose on you—which makes him your enemy as well. He arranged to have me sent out here on a ticklish assignment, hoping to see me fail so he could have my head for it!

"Now, there's the whole picture."

Bannister regarded him for a long moment. "I begin to understand. You're saying that, for my own good, I had damn well better see to it you *don't* fail. Even if it means sacrificing those men on Turkey Ridge to the syndicate . . ."

"You don't really trust me at all, do you?"

"I'm trusting you with my life," Jim Bannister pointed out. "It's your business methods I don't know about."

"And those people you're shedding tears over, those men on the Ridge—it doesn't matter that they're lying their heads off, to alibi someone who tried to kill us both?"

The tall man shrugged. "Desperate men will do a lot of things."

"I'm somewhat desperate myself, Bannister. Or I wouldn't ask you to help. . . ."

There could be no denying the man's sincerity when he said that, at least. Scowling, Jim Bannister paced to a window and looked into the busy street, hearing the rumble of traffic outside and the busy ticking of a clock on the doctor's mantelpiece—forced to admit he was too deeply indebted to Boyd Selden to refuse. With the feeling of a man trapped in something against his will, he swung back.

"All right," he said shortly. "You win. Just try not to forget that my name is Bowers, not Bannister. . . ."

At once Selden's manner changed; he appeared highly pleased—very much the way he must look, Bannister couldn't help supposing, when he had put over an advantageous point in some complicated business deal. His hand still shook a bit as he fumbled a thin gold watch from his pocket and looked at it, comparing it with the clock on the mantel.

"One thirty," he said. "In half an hour I have a meeting with J. T. Herron, in Herron's office. I wish I knew where that boy is, with my other clothes from the hotel room." He stuffed the watch away, nodded toward the window. "How long since your animal has had a decent feed of oats?"

"It's been a while," Bannister admitted.

"Take him over to the Wideawake Livery and fix him up; tell them to put it on my bill. Then hurry back—with this arm, I'll need help getting dressed."

"All right," Bannister said again. He looked at Selden and there was a touch of irony in his words as he answered, "Whatever you say, boss . . ."

CHAPTER VI

To be on the dodge meant living off the country. It meant living lean, traveling often and fast and at a moment's notice, and for long stretches without letup. It was tough on a man and could be even harder for his horse. He could use up a lot of horses, traveling that lonely trail. And each one he lost was like losing a friend.

Jim Bannister had owned the dun for only a few weeks but already he knew it well—its strengths and weaknesses, and the extra bit of heart that would keep it going after many another horse might have given up and quit. As long as it had anything left, he knew he could call on it and the dun would give to the point of dropping in its tracks. Just now, thinning flanks and a rough coat told of how the animal had been faring, and one advantage that would come from the enforced stay in Silver Hill was that Bannister's mount, at least, would have a chance to fill its belly with good and plentiful grain.

It seemed to appreciate the manger that he filled for it, and tied into the food while Bannister lingered to check its hoofs and a spot on its withers where the blanket had threatened to rub.

Bannister gave the hostler careful orders for a good rubdown and further feedings. Afterward, with a parting slap on the rump, he left his animal in the barn and made his way back through town to rejoin Boyd Selden at the doctor's office.

Always uneasy in a crowd, or on strange streets, he walked cautiously and with a constantly moving glance that hunted every face, and every half-seen movement, for any hint of danger. Even so, a man could not be conscious of everything. When a voice behind him said pleasantly, "Hello, Jim!" he was caught unaware, in mid-stride. He stiffened. His pulse lurched and he turned in such haste that he almost stumbled before he caught his balance, with one hand striking the butt of the holstered gun.

He searched and quickly found the man who had emerged from the dark cave of a cheap gambling hall's entrance. There was a dry humor in the voice that warned him, "Careful—you'll tangle in your own spurs! I never knew a big man yet that wasn't clumsy. . . ."

His name was Clee Dorset, and he was anything but big. Probably he would have measured less than average height, and he had a fine-boned wiriness that made him look even smaller. Nothing about him would have stood out, not the ordinary-looking face nor the commonplace denim jacket and jeans, not even the gun in a brush-scarred holster; you had to look closely, and see the opaque and depthless surface of the eyes that never seemed to blink, before you were apt to doubt your first impression. For Bannister knew that those hands, as slender as a girl's, were deadly both with the gun and with the slim-bladed knife he carried in a sheath at the back of his neck.

He had killed with both weapons. Also, he had robbed banks, held up more than one stagecoach, and stolen horses and cattle when occasion arose. His lawlessness rode lightly on the man's slim shoulders, which could shrug aside the weight of it with no trace of concern. Bannister, who had crossed his trail by pure accident, knew the man was completely amoral; though by his own standards he would probably have claimed he had a conscience, and a code.

Easing out of the doorway now, he came to a stand beside the taller man where their talk would travel no farther than their own ears. He measured the size of the other and said coolly, "I sure didn't expect I'd be meeting *you* here. Never really expected to see you again, in fact. When was it you walked in on my campfire, and we got acquainted? A year ago?"

"A bit over," Jim Bannister said. "I'd say closer to a year and a half."

"Guess that would be right." The other nodded. "When you dropped out of sight last winter I was sure something had happened to you, or else you'd left the country; but, I see you're still staying ahead of them. Ain't you kind of stretching your luck this time, though?"

By showing himself openly on the streets of Silver Hill, he meant. Jim Bannister answered, "I could ask you the same question."

The smaller man shrugged. "That's different. Nobody wants me twelve thousand dollars' worth. Anyway, I'm no hulk of a giant that people are apt to remember, or look at twice. Ordinary, is the word for me. When I get tired of trail rations and using a rock for a pillow—or feel the urge to look at a few rounds of stud poker—I find it's generally safe enough to lose myself in a town, provided I don't stay too long." He measured Bannister with his opaque black eyes. "For you, though, I don't think it would ever be safe."

"I suppose it isn't. But I had no choice. I had business in Silver Hill."

"Seems like I been hearing something about that business! There's a rumor that some fellow got his chips cashed for him, earlier today. Description of the one that tagged him sounded damned familiar—big, yellow-haired bastard, I was told. At the time I thought, 'It couldn't really be!' Was I wrong?"

Bannister neither confirmed nor denied it. He said merely, "You're apt to hear almost anything, around a camp like this one." In no mood to prolong this he added shortly, "Well, watch your step," and started to move away.

The opaque stare showed nothing of what lay behind it. "You better do the same. . . ." Bannister thought he could feel the eyes on his back, following him until the busy press of traffic swallowed him up.

It was a chilling discovery, to know someone here knew him by sight. If Clee Dorset, why couldn't there be others? As far as that went, how could he be sure the outlaw himself wouldn't find that twelve thousand bounty too much of a temptation? Because they had once shared grub and a campfire, didn't necessarily make him a friend. . . .

"The J. T. Herron Building," Boyd Selden commented, as the turning of a corner brought it into view. "This should tell you who's the important man in Silver Hill."

Bannister eyed the massive pile of stone and shining window glass, covering almost half a city block and rising a full story higher than its tallest neighbors; but he took a sharper interest, just then, in the clot of men grouped outside the entrance of a clapboard saloon across the street. He counted four, and recognized them as some of the Turkey Ridge miners who had watched him kill Ed McIver. Their intent reaction was plain, as one caught sight of the pair on the opposite walk and called the others' attention.

"I see them," Boyd Selden said before Bannister could speak. "Keep your eyes open!"

"And be ready to earn my hundred bucks?" Bannister added dryly. He could almost feel the hostility beating at them across the rutted dirt. He motioned his companion ahead, to take a lead of a pace or two which gave himself room for action, and loosened his gun in the holster, deliberately making sure those men yonder saw the gesture. His stare sent them a challenge; but even though two wore guns, he didn't feel that any of them were willing, just now, to make the first move against him. Still, his hand rode close to his own filled holster as he moved on behind the syndicate man.

It was probably lucky, he thought, that Lewt Flagg—McIver's tough and militant partner— didn't happen to be there; with him present, there might have been no way to forestall a triggering of some kind of explosion. But the seconds ticked by, and he and Selden drew abreast of the group and then were past it, Bannister keeping them in the tail of his eye. Presently he saw one swing his arms angrily, wrench about and go stomping inside the saloon, and a moment later the others broke and straggled after him. And knowing the danger—for the moment—had passed, Jim Bannister shrugged the tension from his shoulders.

As he pulled up into step with Boyd Selden the latter nodded and said briefly, "Fair enough, Bannister. You see now, I was wise to hire a bodyguard."

The tall man had no comment.

They crossed a cindered alleyway and came to the big stone block of the Herron Building. The ground floor held business establishments—a barbershop, a clothing store, a billiard room through whose open doors Bannister caught a glimpse of richly polished wood and gilt-framed paintings and some of what must be Silver Hill's wealthier citizens drinking at an ornate bar. The corner of the building, where it faced on two joining streets, was all plate glass that must have cost a fortune to freight in over the mountain roads from Denver; this housed the Bank of Silver Hill, with impressive-sounding assets stenciled on the window.

Boyd Selden turned in through a doorway, flanked by bastard Greek pillars; Jim Bannister held back. "You don't need me up there, do you?"

"I want you to meet this man," Selden told him. "You won't have to say anything. I'd be curious for you to listen to him, and tell me how you make him out."

Reluctantly, Jim Bannister let himself be conducted up two flights of stairs to the top floor, and through another door that had J. T. Herron's name stenciled on the pebbled glass. A gray-faced man wearing an eyeshade and black sleeve protectors perched in front of a high desk, working on a ledger. He started to scramble down from his stool, but an inner door stood open and a voice called, "Selden? That you? Come in—come in." Selden gave the clerk a nod, and ushered Bannister ahead of him into the private office of J. T. Herron.

It was richly paneled and carpeted, and twice as large as it needed to be; its very size engulfed the massive furnishings—overstuffed leather chairs, a big globe on a stand, a gleaming mahogany desk. The latter commanded a view out of three windows, over the camp and the circling mountains scarred by the mine workings that were busily tearing the metal ore from them. Two of the walls held maps, one the State of Colorado and the other the Silver Hill mining district; the latter was studded with colored pins.

The man behind the desk seemed dwarfed by his surroundings; having called the invitation, he was frowning now as he saw the stranger who entered with Boyd Selden. Approaching the desk across acres of maroon carpeting, the syndicate man was saying, "J. T., this is Mr. Bowers—a colleague. . . ."

"We were just talking about you, Mr. Bowers," Flora Gentry exclaimed before J. T. Herron could speak.

She had been standing by the desk and she

advanced to meet them, smiling, with a forthright stride that was almost like a man's. "You too, Mr. Selden!" She seized his hand while her brown eyes gave him an appraising look. "I'm glad to see you back on your feet."

"I'm glad to thank you for the help you gave," Boyd Selden answered. "At the time, I'm afraid I wasn't too coherent."

She dismissed that with a flirt of her head, and turned an appraising glance on Jim Bannister. He was conscious, as before, of the way he towered above her. She said, "I hear you've been busy, since I left you two at the doc's! Tom Slate says you already hunted out the man that shot up your boss, and finished him." Her glance touched on the holstered gun. "Well, I figured you didn't wear that just for looks!"

Small as she was she overpowered him just a little, with her doll-like prettiness and candid brown eyes and her mind that had its tough, common streak. Bannister was spared the need of answering when the man at the desk said irritably, "Now Flora, honey, these gents are here to talk business—not to discuss a shooting that ain't a bit of our concern."

"Are you so sure it ain't?" Flora Gentry retorted. She shook her head at him. "I keep telling you: This is a rough camp, made up of tough men. If they once start shooting down people they don't happen to like, chances are there won't be too many names ahead of yours on the list!"

But she didn't argue the point. Turning to Jim Bannister she touched him lightly on the chest and said, "Maybe I'll see you around some more, Mr. Bowers. You too, Mr. Selden. You watch out for that arm, now." She blew a kiss toward the man at the desk. When she left a moment later, with a twirl of her parasol and a flounce of skirts, it was as though a brightly plumaged bird had left the office.

J. T. Herron said, "You do look a little peaked, Selden. Maybe you ought to set." He included Bannister in his gesture toward a couple of heavy leather armchairs that faced the big desk. His visitors came the rest of the distance into the room and settled themselves, Selden with a brief grimace of pain. They looked across the shining expanse of mahogany, at the kingpin of Silver Hill.

CHAPTER VII

Selden had told Bannister, "Whatever he may try to make you think, Herron knows next to nothing about mining. He's an ignorant opportunist who got his start as a bartender, trading free shots of his employer's whiskey to drunken prospectors in return for the paper on their claims. Naturally most of the claims were worthless, but at last he got his hands on one that turned into the Peerless mine, over at Leadville, and made him a millionaire in little more than a year.

"Since then, J. T. Herron hasn't seemed able to lay his hands on anything without it bringing him a fortune. But the fact is, the man's still barely literate—as he was five years ago when he was swabbing down bars and washing glassware, for a bed and three meals a day. . . ."

Bannister's first thought was that Herron reminded him slightly of a spaniel. His face drooped, his eyelids drooped, and so did the ends of a luxurious black mustache that covered much of the lower part of his face. The hair on the top of his head, by contrast, was mostly gone. He was dressed to match his surroundings, his tweed coat carefully tailored and his flowing cravat holding a stickpin that shot forth diamond-sharp gleams at every move. His eyes, a shade too close together, showed a look of concentration and almost of puzzlement, as though J. T. Herron still did not quite comprehend the good fortune that had skyrocketed him to wealth after a lifetime of failure and mediocrity.

But if he was slow-witted, success had made him wary. He sat deep in the padded swivel chair, watching his visitors while he fiddled with a chunk of raw silver on the watch chain that drooped across the front of his waistcoat. His voice held a New England twang as he told Boyd Selden, "After what happened I wasn't sure if you'd be able to make it or not. Anyway, I told my general manager, Miles Kimrey, to sit in with us."

Bannister looked around quickly. He had completely missed the man seated unobtrusively in one of the heavy armchairs, over against the windows. He could see little of him against the bright glare of window light, and this made him acutely uneasy. During the scene that followed he was highly conscious of that dim and silent figure, aware that he was being scrutinized by someone he could not see in turn.

J. T. Herron told the syndicate man, "You asked for this meeting. You got the floor."

"I was hoping you'd reached a decision, on

our preliminary talk the other morning," Selden answered.

"About selling you the Teakettle?" The man behind the desk lifted one shoulder. "I think I told you I ain't in no great rush. I've sunk considerable into developing that property, and lately it's been paying off pretty good—particularly since we hit that likely lookin' vein of silver, down on the third level."

"I know all about that," Selden told him. "I have the report our own experts made when they inspected the property for us."

Miles Kimrey spoke up, from the depths of his chair by the window. In the shadows he appeared slight of body, almost hollow chested; but his voice held the weight and authority of one used to giving orders to a crew and having them carried out. He said, "You remember them syndicate hotshots, J. T. You told me to give 'em the run of the property, and I showed 'em around myself. They seen the new vein. They sounded impressed."

Herron nodded, absently. "I remember." He selected a cheroot from a carved wooden humidor, bit off the end and fished a sulphur match from his waistcoat pocket. "But I figure it's too early to tell, yet, what Turkey Ridge is gonna do. No reason it shouldn't produce at least as well as the rest of this lode. I ain't too much inclined to let go of my piece of it, not just yet."

"Nevertheless, you did promise to have some production figures got ready for me to look at. . . ."

"Oh, them." Herron pulled open a desk drawer, took out a sheaf of papers and skidded them across the polished surface toward his caller. "It's all there," he said casually. "Six months' operation—production reports, smelter receipts, the works."

As Selden studied the figures, Herron snapped the match on a horny thumbnail and puffed the cheroot to light; but Bannister noticed that he never took his look from the syndicate man. For Bannister it was all strangely fascinating—a glimpse into a world of high finance, well beyond his own experience—to sit and listen to these men dicker for a silver mine worth millions, as casually as if it were some fifty-dollar horse. As nothing else ever had, it gave him a real sense of the power of the corporation that he had been trying to combat, with nothing more than the strength of his own two empty hands. . . .

Selden's expert eye seemed to require hardly more than a glance to grasp what he wanted from the figures. Laying the papers on his knee he said, "I came prepared to talk business, on the terms that were mentioned the other morning."

The close-set eyes narrowed; the drooping brows lowered to a scowl. "Well, now," Herron said, in his nasal Yankee speech, "I'd almost rather talk business than eat—but first you got to come up some on the price. Hell, you know that wasn't no sensible offer!"

"It was a very good offer—better than I realized when I made it." If Bannister expected the syndicate man to show temper, he was mistaken. He went on, calmly enough, "I think you may have guessed that my company isn't interested in the Teakettle by itself, but in taking over the development of all Turkey Ridge. And just now we seem to be running into a little difficulty." He touched the bandage on his shoulder.

"Now, hold on!" J. T. Herron sat abruptly forward. "Don't try using that to beat me down! I'll never believe that outfit of yours can be scared off by one sorehead with a rifle! It ain't the syndicate's way. Hell, they flatten resistance—like this gunslinger of yours flattened Ed McIver!" He stared in Bannister's direction.

This time Selden's cheeks colored faintly. He retorted, "We're not discussing the company! We're talking about the offer I made for your Teakettle mine."

"Funny—I can't seem to hear a word you're saying!"

Selden began to drum his fingers on the chair arm, a soundless tattoo. "If you don't like my terms, perhaps you'd like to suggest some."

"Me?" Rolling the cigar between his lips, J. T. Herron shook his head. "You're the one

79

came looking to make a deal. I just been doing you a favor by listening. And I've heard nothing yet that makes any sense."

Boyd Selden studied him a moment longer. "I see. In that case," he said bluntly, "it would appear to be a deadlock." He rose abruptly, and laid the papers on the desk. "I'm sorry to have wasted time for both of us; it begins to look as though there's nothing for my company in this camp after all. And I'm due in San Francisco early next week . . ."

Bannister, watching the man behind the desk, saw him hesitate a moment. It was a moment only. Then Herron said, indifferently, "Suit yourself. But you won't get a stage out of here before tomorrow afternoon, so you might as well take them things along with you and give 'em a closer look." He indicated the papers, with a gesture of the cigar. "They might inspire you."

"It's highly unlikely." But with a shrug Boyd Selden reclaimed the papers and thrust them into a pocket. He looked at Bannister, who had also risen. The interview was clearly over; the visitors got their hats from a table near the door, and a minute or two later were out of the office.

"What do you think?" Selden asked pleasantly. "Does he want a deal?"

"Sure he does," Bannister said. "It was obvious, when he insisted you take another look at those papers. He wants the door left open, all right."

Selden chuckled. He seemed in the best of moods. "So you saw that? You'll make a businessman yet, Bannister!"

"I hope to hell not!" the tall man said gruffly, as they dropped down the dark staircase toward the light and bustle of the street. "All this backing and filling, trying to force the other fellow to tip his hand! I'm a simple fellow. I'd rather do my dealing straight off the top of the deck."

"Or over the barrel of a gun?" Selden suggested.

"If it has to come to that, yes!"

"At least, by now you must have seen which way pays off best." Seldon added slyly, with a sidelong look, "That young widow I met, over in Morgantown—that Mrs. Stella Harbord: she might not see things as you do."

Halting abruptly, Bannister turned to stare at the other. He said coldly, "You better say what you mean!"

The syndicate man appeared taken aback. "Why, I'm not sure I meant anything! Except there can hardly be a woman alive who wouldn't prefer her man to be a success—in my sense of the word—instead of a—"

"A fugitive?" Bannister finished for him, his voice and eyes like stone. "With little chance of ending up anywhere except the end of a rope? That's what you're thinking, isn't it? And who gave you the idea I was her man?"

Boyd Selden met the angry regard of the tall

man's pale eyes. "Oh, come now, Bannister! I'd have to be a fool to miss it. All I had to do was talk with her a minute." He added quickly, "I meant no disrespect. Mrs. Harbord impressed me as a fine young woman!"

Jim Bannister considered the answer, and then with a curt nod turned away and strode into the street, Boyd Selden quickly catching up.

There was no sign of the Turkey Ridge men. As they turned in the direction of the hotel, Bannister asked, "What's the program?"

"We wait. Herron will come around to my terms tomorrow," Selden told him confidently.

"Meaning that I'm stuck in this camp for tonight?"

"Don't forget, it's important to you that I do the job I came for. Besides, there surely won't be any more trouble. . . ."

"If you had thought that," Jim Bannister retorted, "you wouldn't have held me here!" And the other man had no answer.

Miles Kimrey, having watched Selden and the stranger pass from sight in the street below, turned scowling from the window. On his feet, he was a somewhat taller man than Bannister had judged him—clean-shaven, strong-featured, with a restless eye and a neatness about his compactly built frame in its corduroy coat and stag trousers, high boots and flannel shirt open at the throat.

He looked at his employer and there was small respect in his voice as he said, "I'd like to know what you think you're up to!"

Feet on the desk, fingers laced together behind his head, J. T. Herron puffed a cloud of blue smoke around the cigar clamped between his jaws. "What does it look like? I'm unloading worthless property."

"But not to some fool, that don't know the score. Those syndicate men are smart—a hell of a lot smarter than you'll ever be. And they're tough!"

"You trying to scare me?" Herron countered blandly. "You sound like Flora! Maybe you think Selden will send that big gunfighter after me?"

"He won't have to! Whatever made you hand over those phony production figures? Those things are dynamite! They could jail you!"

For just a moment the other's smug confidence seemed shaken. Herron took the cigar from his mouth as he looked at his manager. "You think so?" But then he shrugged off the suggestion. "Hell! As long as I own the smelter, there isn't any way they can prove the mine didn't just suddenly go into borrasca. It's happened before." He wagged his head. "I still think you're just trying to scare me."

"Sometimes I think you're too dumb to scare!" Kimrey stood with feet apart and hands behind his back, eyeing his chief with something near to open contempt. "And while we're at it, just why do you want to let that Chicago outfit get such a toehold for, anyhow? If somebody's going to take over and develop Turkey Ridge, why not us?"

J. T. Herron looked the way his cigar was burning. "Oh, I don't know. After seeing how the Teakettle performed, I ain't sure any of that ridge is worth the trouble. Especially not the kind of trouble Selden seems to be stirring up for himself!"

"One thing certain: Once the syndicate is allowed to move in here, they'll take over. Do you want that? You've been the big frog in this puddle. You'll end up looking like one pretty small toad!"

J. T. Herron cocked a look at his manager, through the blue drift of smoke. "Frankly, that don't bother me a hell of a lot. Far as I'm concerned the syndicate can have Silver Hill—this camp ain't going to hold me forever. I've got ambitions, Miles; I'm meant for bigger things."

"Yeah? What, for instance?"

"Maybe the State House in Denver, for one. Or even Washington."

"You?" The other man gave an incredulous snort. "Don't make me laugh!"

"I'm dead serious." J. T. Herron stabbed the soggy end of his cigar at him, for emphasis. "Silver, and me—don't you go selling us short! I'm riding the crest of the silver boom, and before

I'm done it can wash me clean into the Senate chamber!"

He had Miles Kimrey staring at him. "You think you're going to *buy* your way in? Even *you* haven't got that much money!"

The other didn't even seem to hear. The narrow-set eyes held a feverish gleam that somehow lighted up the whole drooping, spaniel face. J. T. Herron said in an earnest tone, "When I think where I started, and how far I've come, it almost scares me! I can just see us at one of them White House shindigs: Me in a tailcoat, and Flora in that red velvet dress I bought her—fit to knock all them people's eyes out . . ."

Miles Kimrey made a face and shook his head. He turned and walked out of the office and left his chief surrounded by his wealth and by a wreath of blue cigar smoke—gazing through the window at the rimming peaks or, more likely, at his own pleasant fantasies.

CHAPTER VIII

After the scene in Herron's office, it was clear to Jim Bannister that Boyd Selden had been going on nerve and overtaxed strength; by the time they reached his hotel room the man was shaking with fatigue, and his shoulder evidently pained him badly. But Selden declared he would be all right after a thorough rest. There were no other meetings, no further business he had to attend to that day. He would sleep, and have a meal sent up later. Bannister was free to do whatever he wanted.

He found himself at loose ends. He spent an hour in the hotel lobby writing a letter to Stella Harbord at Morgantown, not knowing when he would have another such opportunity. Finished, he dropped the envelope in the mail slot at the desk and then went into the dining room for an early supper, choosing a corner table that put a solid wall behind him and gave him a view of both the kitchen door and the tasseled archway that led into the lobby.

The food was good and he ate with real enjoyment; by the time he finished, the room was still no more than half-filled and no one had showed him undue interest. Going through the town to the livery stable to check on his horse, he then returned to the hotel and, seated in a cane rocker on the deep veranda, rolled and smoked a couple of cigarettes while the swift mountain twilight descended on Silver Hill.

Tom Slate came by along the sidewalk, saw him and turned up the veranda steps to halt before his chair, hands rammed into trouser pockets. "I was looking for you," Slate said with his usual bluntness.

"Were you?"

The constable's face, in the deepening shadows, was unreadable. "Been talking to the judge about the McIver shooting. He didn't like it a bit. He was inclined to call for a full-scale hearing, but after all I was an eyewitness and I testified that it was self-defense. The judge has got a full docket as it is; I persuaded him to let the matter go. It would have been a nuisance."

Bannister released the breath he had been holding. "Then do I take it you're not interested in me anymore?"

Perhaps he only imagined that Slate was a trifle slow to answer. "Not in the McIver shooting," the constable said, his eyes still pinned on the man seated before him. He added, "You expect to be around a few days?"

"That's up to Selden. He's my boss, you know."

The other nodded shortly. "So he says."

With hardly any more than that, he swung away and tramped down the veranda steps. Jim Bannister was left staring after him, narrow-eyed, wondering if there had been something hidden behind his words. And the last golden patina of sunset faded off the barren ridges and darkness flowed through the town.

It scarcely altered its tempo with the coming of night. The stamps continued their pounding. Night shifts took over at the mines, whose tunnel mouths were marked out by clusters of lights that came to life along the ridge faces; on the flats below the town, the smelters now put forth a lurid glow. If anything, Bannister thought the life here took on an even more frantic pace as saloons and gambling joints and brothels tuned up for the evening's business.

His cigarette finished, he stubbed it out against the porch railing and swung to his feet, shivering as the chill struck through him. He entered the hotel, through the lamp-lighted lobby and up the stairs, turning at the corridor to the room he had taken adjoining Selden's. And as he turned the corner, he was startled to catch sight of someone crouching in front of the syndicate man's closed door.

For all Bannister could tell in that first unexpected glimpse, he could have been working at the lock, or trying to peer through the keyhole. At the sound of footsteps, the man's head jerked around and the spray of light from a wall lamp showed blinking, red-rimmed eyes, and cheeks shagged with whisker stubble. Then, with an angry shout, Bannister was on him and he lurched to his feet.

He looked like a derelict; his clothes stank and the taller man caught the sour whiskey breath that gusted from him. But at some time he must have been a fighter, because he aimed a wicked fist at the throat that, had it landed, could have done real damage. Bannister managed to jerk aside in time and the fist barely grazed his collarbone, jarring a grunt of surprise from him.

The man didn't appear to be armed and Bannister left his own gun in its holster. He deflected the knee that tried to take him in the groin and his open palm cuffed the other severely, across the whiskered jaw, jerking his head around and slamming his shoulders hard against the closed door. A whining sound broke from the man and he came bouncing off the panel, lowering his head and trying to ram his way past his opponent and escape.

Bannister would not allow it. He seized the derelict by his filthy coat collar, spun him, and, grabbing an arm, forced it up between his shoulders. "If you're not a fool," he said roughly, "you'll quit!"

At once the fellow gave up and turned docile, shaking violently in Bannister's grasp and whimpering a little. Now a key rattled in the lock and the door opened to show Boyd Selden's startled face and the glint of a small-caliber pistol in his hand. Bannister shoved past him, hustling his prisoner inside, and Selden quickly shut the door again and locked it. Releasing his grip, Bannister thrust the derelict away, hard, so that he stumbled and barely kept his feet. Selden still held the gun. He demanded, "What's going on?"

"That's what I intend for him to tell us!"

The man seemed to have lost all his nerve. Slack lips trembling, he tried to speak but ended by pointing dumbly toward the bottom of the closed door; Bannister looked and saw the fold of paper that had been slid underneath and lay on the faded carpet. "So *that's* what you were up to!" he grunted.

He leaned for it, found Boyd Selden's name penciled on the outside fold and handed the paper over to the syndicate man. Laying aside his gun, Selden glanced over the note and returned it without comment to Bannister; the latter read:

> The whole camp knows you're being played for a sucker. Before you let Herron sell you a pig in a poke, make them show you what happened on that third level.

There was no signature. Bannister looked at the prisoner.

"You wrote this?"

The man found his tongue. His voice had a painful whiskey hoarseness. "Me? Hell, I cain't even read!"

"There's no question at all," Boyd Selden put in, "it came from that Turkey Ridge crowd. Somebody obviously thinks that if I'm told there's been trouble at the Teakettle, I'll lose all interest in it and in the Ridge."

"'The whole camp knows,'" Bannister read aloud. "Might there really be something to it?"

"It doesn't jibe at all with the figures Herron gave me—but, figures can be doctored. The point is, my orders from the company aren't changed. To the contrary: Whatever they intended, if there's anything in this it actually strengthens my hand."

"How do you mean?"

"Why, I've had a feeling all along that Herron was bluffing, with poor cards. This would explain it. It would also mean I can afford to hold out for almost any price I feel like giving him. Provided, of course," the syndicate man added quickly, "the writer of the note knows what he's talking about—and something *has* gone wrong with that big strike. . . ." And his stare turned again to the prisoner who had stood snuffling and trembling, forgotten for the moment.

Bannister also looked at him. "Well? If you didn't write this—who did? Where did you get it?"

The man cringed as though expecting another blow. "I dunno anything, mister! Honest to God! I only drifted into this camp today. I was lookin' around, trying to raise the price of a drink, and there was this bird said he'd give me a dollar if I was to get into the hotel without being seen, and slip a paper under the door that he told me the number of."

"Go on—what did he look like?"

"It was gettin' late," the prisoner explained in a whine. "I couldn't see much of him at all, except that he was pretty big. Not big like you, maybe, but big enough."

Bannister thought, Lewt Flagg? But he kept the notion to himself as he glanced silently at Boyd Selden. The latter was not satisfied. He shook his head and said with determination, "This isn't good enough. It's important that I know the writer before I can decide if there's anything here to act on." And Bannister, taking that as an order, reluctantly nodded. Without much taste for this, he turned again to the prisoner.

"You got a name?"

"Sharkey—just Bill Sharkey. That's me, mister." His face twisted into a grimace that tried to be an ingratiating smile. "Never hurt nobody in my life!"

"That's good. Do as you're told now, Sharkey, and maybe nobody will hurt *you*. Understand?"

The man swallowed. "What you want of me?"

"I think you said you haven't been paid yet?" And as the other shook his head: "Then I'll just go along with you while you collect, and have a look at this fellow."

"No!" The protest exploded in a gust of whiskey breath. "If he sees somebody with me, he'll never even show! I won't get a dime!"

"He won't see me," Bannister promised curtly. And Boyd Selden, with a sour look, dug into a pocket and brought out a golden double eagle which he held up before the derelict.

"This change your mind any?"

Bill Sharkey's eyes bulged. "Hell, yes!"

He started to reach for the coin but Selden flipped it instead to Bannister, a golden streak of light. "Give it to him when you're satisfied he's shown you the right man."

"You see how it is," Bannister told the prisoner. "Play your hand right, and you get paid twice. It's up to you." Bill Sharkey watched hungrily as the coin disappeared into the tall man's pocket.

He was still shaken, still trembling. He made a last effort. "I could sure use a drink. Cain't you let me have just one drink first?"

With ill-concealed disgust, Jim Bannister turned to the dresser, uncorked the bottle that stood there and poured two scant fingers of whiskey into a water glass. The prisoner snatched it from him and threw the liquor down his throat, gagging pitifully as the fire of it hit him. Afterwards he obeyed meekly enough when Bannister unlocked the door and motioned him through ahead of him.

The stars were out, glittering like lamps in the black mountain sky, except where the newly risen moon turned them pale. Down here in the streets of Silver Hill, roof lines and building corners made inky silhouettes; the dust of the narrow side street where Bill Sharkey led Bannister showed almost milky white, as it ran down a shallow hill to the crossing with the busy main thoroughfare.

"You're sure this is the right place?" Bannister demanded.

Sharkey insisted it was. "I was told to wait right here when I'd delivered the note, and he'd be along."

"All right."

It looked as likely a place as any. The buildings were mostly dark, only one or two windows showing lamplight; the dust was undisturbed by any of the traffic that moved along the main street, a short half block below.

"What you want me to do when he comes?"

"You don't have to do anything," Bannister said. "This moonlight ought to give me a fair look at him—though you might try to get him talking so I can hear what his voice sounds like. As soon as he's paid you and left, you get the gold piece. No reason to be nervous," he added. "No one's going to get hurt."

94

Bill Sharkey was still unconvinced, but without arguing he took his place on a wooden bench fronting a deserted blacksmith's shop. The building next to it might also have been deserted; it had a bootmaker's sign, and a wooden awning that threw the boardwalk in front of it into dark shadow. Jim Bannister stationed himself in the recessed doorway, thinking he could see whatever happened from there without being conspicuous.

Almost immediately he tensed, as someone turned the corner and started briskly toward him, footsteps rattling the loose sidewalk plankings. Bill Sharkey had heard, too, and he came off his bench to stand waiting expectantly. Lost in shadow the man drew nearer, finally passing so near to Bannister that the latter might have reached out and touched him. He walked out from under the arcade's shadow, into moonlight—and without a glance for Sharkey continued up the hill and so out of sight. And Bannister let go of the air he had trapped in his lungs.

The wrong man . . .

Sharkey had already dropped back onto his bench again; Jim Bannister settled into the collar of his windbreaker, for the night was turning colder, with a chill wind off the peaks. He found himself growing irritable. No telling how long Bill Sharkey might be kept waiting for his dollar, if he ever got paid at all, and meanwhile Bannister could think of any number of places better than this; only the direct order from Boyd Selden held him where he was.

If there was anything at all behind the hint contained in that note, it was probably nothing more than hearsay and public rumor; even nailing the writer would not be likely to gain Selden much. And if it should turn out to be Lewt Flagg, or one of his friends, Bannister strongly disliked the thought of starting more trouble with the Turkey Ridge miners. They were men caught in a squeeze play between selfish and powerful interests, and he couldn't help but feel a certain kinship with them.

He was debating with himself, nearly ready to back out of this, when he became aware of a glimmer of light beyond the door beside him. Turning, he peered through dirty glass and saw an old man with a painful stooped shuffle enter the shop through a rear door, carrying a lighted lamp past bins and workbenches cluttered with finished boots and tools and scraps of leather. He placed the lamp in a wall holder near the door and turned back, leaving it there to shine directly in Bannister's eyes. The tall man forgot for the moment that the glow of it must fall directly across his own face; he remembered when a sudden shout went up, near that street crossing a hundred feet below where he stood.

He swore silently and edged out of the light, but a shade too late. Another voice joined the first

96

one and this time he made out the words: "Hey—watch it! Where'd he go to? It was that damned syndicate gunman!" Bannister felt a slight sweat break out on him as he put a hand on his belted gun and drew it partway from the holster. He didn't need to be told he had been spotted by the Turkey Ridge men.

All at once Bill Sharkey was beside him and Bannister heard his harsh question: "What the hell's going on down there?"

"Nothing for you to worry about." But he could smell the fear on the man, and almost feel his trembling.

Below them now there was definite movement in the confusion of shadow and moonlight and streaky lantern glow. A piercing whistle sounded—a signal perhaps? Someone called out in a note of urgency: "Lewt! Lewt Flagg!"

"I'm getting the hell out of here!" Bill Sharkey said.

Bannister exclaimed, "Wait, you fool! It's me they want. . . ." But the other man was already lunging away up the hill, at a shambling, graceless run. As he burst into the open, there was a yell and someone below let loose, startlingly, with a pistol shot.

The explosion and streak of fire shocked the night, and on the heels of the shot the running figure went down. At almost the same moment, the lamp in the building at Jim Bannister's back

97

was hastily extinguished. Sharkey had only stumbled over the ruts, apparently; he came floundering to his feet again and scampered on. Bannister could hear his wind-broken sobs of fright. Then the night swallowed him.

The tall man had pulled his own gun but he still did not use it. Instead he took three sidling steps that moved him along the face of the darkened shop and around its corner. Apparently the movement was seen; a man cried, "There he goes! He's heading for the alley!"

And Lewt Flagg's bull voice answered: "Let's take him—there's enough of us. But be careful of that damned gun!"

Even peaceable men could turn bloodthirsty, Jim Bannister thought bleakly, once they were given provocation and opportunity. Carrying the gun—not wanting to use it, but conditioned by hard experience to defend his own life if he had to—he turned and made his way through the slot between the buildings. At the rear he paused to listen for pursuit, but the steady night wind and the racket of the wide-open silver camp made it hard to sort out and label noises he heard. Going blind, then, he cut left to a small, slant-roofed shed, and looked into the service alley that ran parallel to the town's main street.

Ironic, he thought. Earlier he had herded Ed McIver through the camp's alleys, and now McIver's friends were doing the same to him. . . .

At once he caught a warning and drew back into the scant shadow. Scarcely breathing, he listened to the crunch of footsteps on cinders and now two men hurried by, sprinting, and he caught the liquid glint of moonlight on polished gunmetal. Had one of them turned to look, he could hardly have missed the figure pressed against the shed wall.

As they went on, Bannister heard the thin lift of a shouted question somewhere behind him, and another answering it. They were really hunting him, and making a sober business of it!

So he could not turn back. Ghosting along the rubble-strewn alley, mindful of not overtaking the pair ahead of him, he presently brought up in the shadow of a barn and halted while he keened the busy, windy night. The darkness seemed full of movement, hard to pinpoint. At that moment a horse, stabled within the barn, caught the stranger's scent and moved uneasily about in its stall, a shod hoof striking a timber.

Somebody shouted, "He's after a mount!"

Hurriedly Jim Bannister skirted the shed and ran through the littered yard beyond, toward the black outline of a building that faced on the main street. Constant yelling now. A revolver loosed a pair of hasty shots, and the horse in the shed neighed and lunged against the flimsy walls in terror.

Just at Bannister's left was a shoulder-high

board fence. He leaped at it, vaulted over and landed directly atop a pile of firewood that collapsed and scattered under him. He almost lost his gun as he went sprawling, but held onto it and picked himself up, kicking billets of chopped limb lengths out of his way when they threatened to turn under his boots and throw him a second time. He had narrowly missed spraining an ankle; he was hobbling slightly, favoring his left leg, as he hurried on toward the lights of the main street that glowed, now, ahead of him.

Suddenly he veered aside, hearing heavy cowhide work boots trampling the boardwalk. Coming from two directions, they would shortly have him caught between them. At his left loomed the bulk of a saloon, all its windows lighted and the sound of early evening trade reverberating through the raw timber siding. Then he saw there was a side door, and asking for no more of a break than that he made for it, still hobbling.

The door was unlocked. Bannister slipped inside without pausing, drew it shut while he got his bearings.

Light and sound met him. It was still early and the barroom was a little more than half full, with a couple of bartenders working and a certain amount of activity at the gaming tables. Bannister glanced briefly over the latter, through a gray swirl of tobacco fumes, and his eye held suddenly on a back and a pair of shoulders that were sharply familiar. Then the man turned his head for a moment and he saw it was Clee Dorset, sitting in on a five-handed poker game.

The little outlaw had said that a hankering for stud poker was one of his prime reasons for venturing into Silver Hill, despite its dangers. Clee Dorset had a real taste for gambling, Bannister knew—for big stakes or matchsticks, it made small difference.

Jim Bannister turned to the bar—and instantly saw two other men he knew standing together at one end, talking earnestly over their drinks. They were Turkey Ridge men, that he recognized from the scene in the restaurant—one of them, a quiet, sober-looking man whose name, he remembered, was Jud Murrow. He thought, Then they aren't all out there in the night, hunting me. . . .

But it would not be long before the hunters would track him here. He could not have gone anywhere else—sooner or later the chase would draw them straight to this room. So, he thought grimly, let them find him! Here, in front of witnesses, was a better place than out in one of the camp's black alleys.

Stepping to a vacant place at the counter, Bannister caught a bartender's eye and ordered beer. He put down his money and, facing the bar mirror where he could watch the reflection of both outside doors at once, lifted the schooner. He drank, as he waited for his enemies. . . .

CHAPTER IX

He had to wait hardly any time at all.

Jim Bannister had taken the level of the glass down no more than an inch or two, when his alert senses picked up the sound of several boots striking the porch. Schooner still lifted, he went very still, watching the reflection in the mirror as the street door was abruptly pushed open; Lewt Flagg appeared, a hand on the knob as he checked the room.

He was almost in too great a hurry. His probing look ranged over the bank of card tables, moved to the scattered row of drinkers bellied against the bar. It passed directly over Bannister without seeing him. Flagg had actually turned to leave when, in the mirror, Bannister saw him stiffen. The big miner's head jerked about; his eyes pinned the tall man standing by himself—and this time, apparently, the sight of him registered.

The door flung wide, and Flagg strode through with five of the Turkey Ridge men close behind him. He had a gun engulfed in one big fist. Back muscles gone tight, Jim Bannister stood and forced himself to take another deliberate swallow of the beer, as though oblivious to the danger bearing in his direction.

But now the big fellow's voice boomed through the place, topping every other. "Bowers! God damn you, so I finally run you to earth!" The whole room stilled. Bannister lowered the half-empty schooner; he set it on the bar and turned slowly.

"You were looking for me?" His glance passed to those who had entered the room behind Flagg. "All six of you?"

Flagg's thick shoulders moved angrily. "They don't count," he muttered. "This is between us two!"

"All I see between us is the gun you're holding. And it looks like you're itching to use it."

Jud Murrow, from the end of the bar, exclaimed in horror, "Flagg! His hands are empty! You make a mistake and they'll hang you for it. . . ."

Color flowed into the man's dark face. He let the muzzle of the gun drop, and, at that, some of the constriction eased out of Jim Bannister's chest.

But Flagg made no move to holster the weapon, declaring hoarsely, "No matter what, I ain't taking chances with no syndicate gunslick! An ordinary man hasn't got a prayer, against such as him—poor Ed McIver showed us that. We buried McIver this afternoon, Bowers. But just because you put a man out of sight, under the ground, don't mean he's that easy forgotten. Or that we're forgetting who it was murdered him!"

From his eyes, Bannister knew the big miner had been drinking—likely not sufficient to slow his reactions, but only to make him dangerous. He drew a breath, conscious of the weight of attention resting on the pair of them; he shook his head. "There's no use even discussing this— not if you insist on calling it murder, when the constable himself testified it wasn't."

"When a gunslick kills an ordinary man it's always murder!" Flagg retorted. "But, by God, there are other ways to deal with your kind. . . . Take off that belt and holster."

Not moving, Bannister returned his look coldly. "What now?"

"I said, lay that gun aside and let's see just how big you are without it." He slowly brought up one thick, scarred hand, and folded it into a fist. "We'll use *my* weapons, Bowers. Big as you are, I'll cut you down to size!"

One of the bartenders blurted, "Not in here, damn it!" but Flagg didn't seem to hear. Bannister met the man's wolfish stare; he looked at the revolver that was once more pointed squarely at his middle, and felt a prickling of sweat break out under his shirt. Lewt Flagg, he thought, was just drunk enough—and furious enough—to shoot him down where he stood.

"You got half a minute," Flagg said, "to put your gun on the bar. . . ."

Bannister shrugged resignedly and worked the buckle of his holster belt, laid the belt and gun on the bar and placed his hat beside them. Flagg, as soon as he saw he was to have his way, let his lips spread in a wicked grin; he handed his own weapon to one of his friends—and, without warning, started for Bannister while the latter still had his back half turned.

No one cried out, no one did a thing. But in this stillness, the thump of Flagg's boots betrayed him. A glance into the bar mirror gave Bannister warning. He pivoted just in time. Lewt Flagg ran full tilt into the edge of the bar, with a force that drove a grunt of surprise and pain out of him. And as he came around, Bannister was there to send a fist squarely into his face, rocking him back onto his heels while the hat popped from his head.

The bartender was shouting again, "Outside! *Take it outside!*" No one paid him any attention.

Momentarily stopped, Flagg pawed a hand across his mouth and swore at the sight of his own blood. It was enough to bring him lumbering forward again, both fists swinging. He was an inch or two shorter than his opponent, but with heavy shoulders and unnaturally long arms that gave him a shade more reach. Bannister was able to block the wild blow aimed at his head, and

105

striking past the other's defense felt his knuckles bounce off the heavy muscle of a shoulder. Then Flagg closed with him and the whole room split with excited yelling as the two big men came together, slugging.

It would not be often that they got to see such a pairing of size and bulk. Actually, hampered by the heavy windbreakers worn by both men, a body blow could hardly do much damage; but Lewt Flagg, at least, showed a good knowledge of all the refinements of dirty barroom brawling. He tried to use a knee on Bannister but the latter was able to block it. The taller man was satisfied to give ground while looking for a chance to work on Flagg's face, hoping to hurt him and force a halt to this senseless combat.

Unluckily, in retreating he put his weight for a moment on that weakened left ankle; to a skewering pain he felt the leg give way under him. He twisted violently as he started down. Just behind him, one of the round card tables had been deserted barely in time, the players scrambling out of their chairs as the battle rolled toward them; Bannister struck the edge of it and the table went over beneath his weight, in a scatter of bottle and glasses and cards and poker chips. He hit the floor, on hands and knees.

And big Lewt Flagg, promptly wading in, aimed the swing of a blunt boot toe that caught him squarely in the chest.

The force of the kick lifted Bannister, flung him hard against the upset table. Dazed, feeling his ribs must surely have caved, he reached out and managed to catch hold of his opponent about the legs. Flagg swore, but could not break clear; a sudden wrench made him topple heavily forward, over Bannister's shoulder and squarely across the table's tilted edge.

Jim Bannister was fighting for wind as he climbed to his feet. Flagg had smashed one of the barrel chairs in falling and was sprawled amid the wreckage, feebly struggling to extract himself. Leaning, Bannister laid hold of the man's clothing and hauled him up, and threw a right at the point of the black-stubbled jaw. The big fellow's head jerked sideward and he started to sag. Not letting go, Bannister measured him and struck again, and then stepped back as Lewt Flagg slid limply down the slant of the table to the floor.

Gasping past the lump of agony in his chest where he had been kicked, Jim Bannister raised his head and looked about at the suddenly silent room.

It might have been peopled with statues, every man frozen just as the sudden ending of the fight had caught him. Of them all, only Clee Dorset still remained seated; but even the little gunman seemed unable to move. He appeared to have forgotten the deck of cards he held in one hand.

He returned Bannister's look without expression, or a hint of recognition.

Jim Bannister pushed a hand through the tangle of his hair. Flexing the knuckles of his aching right fist, he turned to the bar, picked up his gun belt and passed it around his waist and buckled it. He took his hat then and, holding it in his hands, sent a look over the faces of the men from Turkey Ridge.

"Bear in mind," he said sternly, "I never wanted this fight—any more than I wanted to shoot McIver. When things are pushed onto a man, he can only push back!" He gave them time to answer, but they still appeared stunned by the swiftness of Lewt Flagg's defeat. Bannister looked at their scowling faces and at the bloody figure sprawled against the overturned table. And he turned and walked out of there, limping slightly on that twisted ankle.

Outside, the cold wind tumbling through the street stung his sweating face. For all its tang of chemicals from the smelter below town, the night air was better than the stale tobacco and whiskey smells he left behind. Breathing deeply, testing the pain in his chest and relieved to find the kick from Flagg's boot had seemingly done no real damage, Bannister brought out a handkerchief and wiped his face, afterward starting in the direction of the hotel.

Silver Hill was never really quiet, at any hour;

but at least there was no threat of danger in the air now. But when he had walked a half block he caught the sound of running footsteps behind him, and caution spun him into deep shadow where he half pulled the gun from his holster.

The footsteps lagged. A voice called anxiously, "Bowers?"

"Who is it?" he challenged.

"Jud Murrow. . . ."

Bannister placed him—the quiet, serious-mannered member of the Turkey Ridge crowd, who had been at the bar when he entered the saloon. He holstered the gun but kept his hand on it as he said gruffly, "All right, come ahead."

He let the man approach, showing up against the night. "That's close enough," he said finally. "What do you want?"

"Don't let mc make you nervous, Mister Bowers," the man said quickly. "I got no gun on me. But I got something on my conscience. I want to tell it."

"Yes?"

Murrow seemed to have trouble getting it out. For a moment there was only the sound of his breathing, harshened by the effort of overtaking the other man. Then he blurted: "I feel like a traitor, almost; but the more I been thinking about it, the surer I am that Flagg and the rest are all mistaken about Ed McIver being with us, this noon. I can't tell you just when he did join us, but

I'm convinced now there *would* have been time for him to throw a shot at Boyd Selden. And if you claim you saw him do it, then I guess I have to believe you!"

"I assure you," Bannister said, "I did see him."

Murrow sounded deeply troubled. "I don't like to think of any of our crowd doing such a thing; all I can figure is that McIver must have been more worked up over the syndicate than any of us knew. I'm just sorry for not speaking earlier."

"No harm done," Bannister said. "Tom Slate believed my version, and so did the judge; so as far as concerns the law, I'm clear. As for those friends of yours, I don't imagine anything could make them change their minds. . . ."

The door of the saloon, a hundred yards away, had been suddenly flung open. A man came staggering out, bellowing with rage, the spill of light from door and window silhouetting him and showing the big, hulking shape of Lewt Flagg. Gunmetal glinted in his hand as he reeled out into the street. "Bowers! You yella dog—come back here and finish this!"

Murrow's breath caught in his throat. "Damn the man!" he exclaimed in a hoarse whisper. "Don't he know when he's whipped?" He added quickly, "You beat him fair! Don't let him goad you."

"That's all right," Bannister assured him. "I'm not in the least tempted!"

Flagg continued to yell his threats, working himself into a frenzy of rage and frustration; plainly he would start shooting at any hint of a target. But now other men had come from the saloon and they surrounded him. There was a sound of argument—the Turkey Ridge men, obviously, were trying to reason with Flagg and calm him.

A swing of the big man's arm put one of them flat in the dust, but now the others had laid hold and, after a moment, he subsided. They took his gun away; a few minutes more of earnest discussion, and they persuaded him to turn back with them into the saloon. The one he had knocked down picked himself up and followed. Bannister heard Jud Murrow let out his trapped breath.

"I dunno," Murrow said shakily. "That Lewt Flagg is a wild man when he's crossed! I think I better get down there—see if I can help with him."

Jim Bannister nodded. He said, "Thanks again for going to the trouble of telling me what you just did. Since I know what you think about me, it was more than I had any right to expect. . . ."

The man was already gone, without an answer.

A familiar-looking carriage and team stood before the hotel entrance, with the black driver waiting motionless and patient as a statue. When Jim Bannister entered the lobby, he saw Flora

111

Gentry at the desk, and the clerk shaking his head in negative answer to something she had asked. Seeing Bannister in the doorway he at once corrected himself, and beckoned. The woman turned as the newcomer approached across the deep-napped, turkey-red carpeting.

The clerk said, "Mrs. Gentry was just asking for you, Mister Bowers."

He had seen her three times today, and each time she was dressed differently. Tonight her gown was black, worked with jet beads across the bosom, full at sleeve and bustle; it set off the whiteness of her skin. Her cloak was extravagantly trimmed with fur; the plume that swept downward from her hat brim was the longest he had seen on her yet.

She settled the furs about her plump shoulders as she watched him come toward her, limping slightly. "Something I can do for you?" he asked.

"I want to talk to you."

"All right."

"Anybody using the parlor?" she asked the clerk. And when he shook his head, she added, "We'll go in there, then. Be sure we're not disturbed. Oh—and have somebody bring in a bottle, Harry."

"Sure thing," Harry agreed.

The parlor, opening off the lobby, was small but as elegantly furnished as the rest of this hotel that belonged to J. T. Herron—more turkey-red drapes and carpeting, polished tables and paneling and painted lamp globes. A log crackled pleasantly in the fireplace. At Flora Gentry's suggestion Bannister closed the sliding door and went to join her where she had made herself comfortable on a horsehair sofa, throwing open her cloak.

Her eyes studied him shrewdly. "Something's happened," she guessed. "You look sort of bunged up around the face, and you're limping."

"A little trouble," he admitted, touching a knuckle to his cheek. "Nothing serious." He looked down at his clothing, that was streaked with drying mud from his spill in the woodpile. "But I'm afraid I may not be quite presentable." She only shrugged at that, and he let himself gingerly onto one of the parlor's leather-covered armchairs and placed his hat on a table beside him. He looked at Flora Gentry, giving her the chance to say what she wanted.

Her abrupt question surprised him. "Just how much does the syndicate pay you, Mister Bowers?"

"It—varies," he answered vaguely.

"All right, *don't* tell me." She sounded a little vexed. "But it happens I got a reason for asking. I want to hire you."

He rather thought he blinked. *"You?"*

"I don't know if I can afford you, of course.

But if it's in reach, I'm willing to match Selden's figure."

They were interrupted. There was a knock at the door and a man in a bartender's white jacket entered with a tray of whiskey and glasses, which he placed on the table. When he had left Bannister busied himself for a moment pouring drinks for them both, handed the woman hers and returned to his chair. He could feel her watching him as he deliberately took his glass and sampled the bar stock. At last, looking at her directly, he said, "So you'd like me to kill someone for you. . . ."

"It's nothing like that!" She was indignant. "For one thing, you don't look to me like a killer, Mister Bowers."

"Really?"

"At least, it was my impression you were only acting as a sort of bodyguard for that man Selden. That's the only reason I'd go out of my way to talk to you."

"Don't tell me you think you need a bodyguard."

"Not for myself," she said quickly.

"I see. . . . For J. T. Herron."

Her generous bosom lifted on a convulsive breath, and suddenly she was trembling so that Bannister thought the whiskey would spill from the glass she held. "I live in dread of something terrible happening to him!" she said, and she sounded very close to tears. "Twice in this last month I—I've dreamt I saw him lying in his coffin!"

Bannister stared at her. Finally he said, gently, as he would to a child, "You surely don't believe in dreams?"

"I can't help it if you think I'm crazy!" she retorted. "But I'm Irish—and my mother had the second sight. I'm scared to death for him," she insisted, in a choked voice. "I know he ain't perfect—I know he's made enemies, some even that wouldn't hesitate to kill him if they had the chance. But he's been good to me, and I love him!" And then her eyes challenged Bannister's as she added, "Maybe you doubt that?"

"Why should I doubt it?" He set his glass aside. "One thing I don't understand, though: If Herron's in need of a bodyguard, why depend on you to find him one? I'd have thought he would take care of it himself."

The brown eyes wavered. "He won't. He thinks it's all nonsense. He just laughs."

"Oh." Bannister frowned and shook his head. "But in that case, I'm afraid you're wasting your time. That's nothing you can force on a man, if he isn't of a mind for it. And it isn't even your responsibility."

"You mean because I'm not his wife? I would be, if that bitch he's married to would only give him the divorce he's been begging her for!" Her voice, that had gone high and harsh with angry feeling, broke off and she colored slightly. She put her drink aside, untasted, and came off the couch drawing her cloak around her. "I guess," she said coldly as Bannister quickly got to his feet, "you've already made it clear you won't help me. If it's the money—"

"It isn't the money," Jim Bannister said quickly. "I have an obligation to Boyd Selden, at the moment. Besides which—well, please believe me, it just isn't possible."

"Very well." Flora Gentry shrugged and settled the wrap about her shoulders. "Thank you for your time."

"My pleasure. And I hope you get over this idea that's worrying you." He saw her eyes, looked into them and read bitterness and a fatalism that was near to despair. Then she swung away, without another word.

Bannister got to the door and opened it for her, and watched her cross the lobby and disappear into the night—in a way, feeling almost sorry for the woman; and yet there was nothing he could have said or done. He turned, with a shake of his head, and under the desk clerk's curious stare moved to the carpeted steps.

He had forgotten Boyd Selden. It occurred to him the syndicate man would still be in his room, still anxiously waiting to hear word of his mission with the derelict, Bill Sharkey.

CHAPTER X

Turkey Ridge, hanging above the camp on the east, kept Silver Hill from receiving the earliest rays of the sun. Even now, at mid-morning, the ridge face itself lay in shadow though the wash of light flowing down from the high peaks opposite had gilded the windows of the town in the gulch below. Boyd Selden had not adjusted to the thin air and the chill of this high country, and Bannister could see him shivering as their horses took them up the switchbacks through a lingering half-twilight.

From here, Bannister thought, there was a kind of beauty even to a place like Silver Hill: Distance hid some of its tawdriness, the morning laid a patina that disguised somewhat the scars of prospect holes and the ugly stumpage where virtually every bit of the timber had been stripped for building and for firewood. The low-hanging fumes from the smelter did not reach this far, while the smoke pillars rising above the pattern of roofs added a charm of their own.

Bannister pointed across the emptiness toward a house that stood apart on its own knob of hill—an imposing structure three stories high, with a windowed turret and a mansard roof; its glass flashed like gold under the strike of the sun. "Somebody has him a nice place there."

Selden looked and nodded. Breath hung in steam before his face as he answered shortly, "Herron's . . . It's not finished—I understand everyone's waiting to see whether he'll have the nerve to move the Gentry woman in and live with her there, in front of the whole town."

"I'd say that was their business," Jim Bannister commented, and let the subject drop. He had told Selden nothing of his talk with Flora Gentry, not seeing that J. T. Herron's possible need of a bodyguard was anything to concern the syndicate man. The latter was troubled enough, over the anonymous note he carried in his pocket.

Though he hadn't said so, the note, beyond any question, was bringing them up here this morning, following this dug road whose hairpin turns must be nearly more than the heavy ore wagons could maneuver. Just now an empty one came lumbering up past them, fighting the grade, and they had to pull wide to give it room; waiting, Jim Bannister found himself fidgeting just a little.

His job would not let him forget that they were riding into the very dooryard of Boyd Selden's personal enemies, who had already tried to kill them both.

The steep ridge face was thickly pocked with

118

workings. Tents, brush shelters and shebangs of every description clustered about the adits and tailings. Lanterns glowed behind canvas, smoke from cook-fires whipped in the wind; somewhere a mule brayed raucously in the chill morning. Bannister noticed that some claims already appeared to have been abandoned as hope and patience gave out, though mostly the optimists prevailed. Nearly everything he saw looked to be a typically small-scale operation. Only one, he was willing to guess, had any real capital behind it: J. T. Herron's Teakettle.

It was situated near the very top of the ridge—a complex of raw-looking work buildings. A barn lantern burned on a pole near the shaft opening, though by now the sun had climbed high enough that a spread of light tumbled down the face of the ridge, and a faint tinge of warmth already was working into the day.

At first they saw no one at all. They rode past the tailings dump and through the usual scattering of trash, approaching the shaft house where a steam-operated lift shuttled working crews into the lower tunnels. As they neared this a man stepped out. He might have been oiling machinery, since he was wiping his hands on a piece of waste as he gave the newcomers a close regard. "Looking for somebody?" he asked. It sounded almost like a challenge.

Selden had halted his livery horse and

Bannister too pulled rein, letting the dun move a little distance to the left so that he had an unobstructed view. Now a second man appeared from somewhere. He stood at a corner of the shed, merely watching, his arms hanging at his sides; the gap of his open coat showed the gun shoved behind his waistband.

Boyd Selden answered the question. "I'd like to see the manager, if he's around. Miles Kimrey."

"And who are you?" the first man said.

"Kimrey knows me."

The man thought this over. Then he turned his head to look at the one by the building corner. A message passed and with a nod the second man swung away and started for a building that appeared to house storage and the mine office.

They waited. The ground shuddered under them as somewhere along the ridge a dynamite charge was touched off; Bannister's horse felt it and stomped uneasily and he laid a hand on its neck to calm it. The first man finished with wiping his hands and tossed the bit of waste aside, while he continued to appraise the visitors with a silent stare.

The door of the office opened just then and Miles Kimrey stepped out; the messenger who was still a half-dozen yards away halted and called something, turning to point at the two horsemen. Kimrey looked in that direction, and

120

coming down the short flight of wooden steps walked briskly toward them. He was bareheaded, a compact figure of a man who looked coolly confident of himself. His hands were shoved carelessly into the pockets of his stag pants and highlights ran along the polished boots with each easy stride.

Halting, he favored Selden with a brisk nod but gave Bannister no more than a long stare. To the syndicate agent he said, "I wasn't looking for you. What's on your mind?"

He managed to give the impression of a busy man, impatient with the interruption, but Bannister had a feeling it was an act and that he was watching his visitors with a shrewd attention. Boyd Selden, for his part, was civil enough with his answer. "I don't mean to take up your time. I was merely thinking I should have a personal look at this property we're discussing."

Kimrey made a gesture. "There's not much to see. These buildings are purely temporary. We're planning a reduction shed, to save the expense of hauling crude ore; but work on that hasn't been started yet."

"The buildings hardly matter," Selden replied. "I'm more interested in what's going on down below. Perhaps you could spare someone for an hour to show us around."

Bannister thought the manager was just a trifle slow in responding. "For any particular purpose? I seem to remember you telling J. T. you didn't personally know too much about mining."

"That's true. I generally rely on expert opinion. But since I'm on the ground—and since Herron did say I'd be welcome. . . ."

"I'm afraid it's out of the question."

"Oh?" Selden's face was smooth and lacking suspicion. "Why is that?"

"We've had a little accident this morning—a cave-in, in one of the laterals, from a misplaced powder charge. We don't know yet the extent of the damage. Until we've got it cleared out and the shoring repaired, I couldn't be responsible for you to go down there."

"I'd take the responsibility," Selden assured him quickly.

The man was adamant. "Do I have to spell it out for you? We've got a hell of a cleanup job facing us. Without a direct order from Herron, this mine is closed to visitors."

"Perhaps I'd better talk to Herron!"

Suspicious anger crackled in Selden's voice; but if Kimrey was concerned he gave no sign of it. He merely shrugged, his manner as smooth as ever. "That's your privilege," he said.

A long moment the syndicate man studied him, a taut muscle moving in his smooth-shaven cheek. Jim Bannister put another look on the pair who hung in the background, watching their boss deal with the visitors. The one with the gun had pulled his coat open now and his thumb was hooked into his belt. Bannister caught the man's stare resting directly on himself, unwavering.

Abruptly, Selden gave his rent horse a jerk with the reins that turned it sharply. He told Miles Kimrey, shortly, "You may be seeing me again." Not waiting for an answer, he started away from there and Jim Bannister quickly fell in behind him.

Before the turns of the trail dropped the mine from sight, Bannister looked back and saw Kimrey and his men standing precisely as they had been, unmoving, watching them go. Bannister grunted sourly and rode up beside the syndicate man. He said, "There was no cave-in."

"Naturally," Selden agreed. "He was improvising for all he was worth. I can just imagine him wondering why I should be interested all of a sudden in making an inspection; all the same he was determined I wasn't to do it. Naturally, he knew I'd want to see the big silver vein at the third level—and it's plain enough now that he'd have nothing at all to show me."

"You're really certain, then, it's a fraud? Herron's rigged his figures, trying to sell you a property that's gone into borrasca?" Bannister frowned. "Surely he knows you could haul him into court for a cleaning?"

"That's hard to say. He could be even stupider than I've thought he was! On the other hand, maybe he has a trick up his sleeve. Somehow I have got to find out which it is."

That made Bannister's head lift and turn to stare. "Are you saying you'd deliberately buy a mine you knew was worthless—just to back someone into a trap? Is *that* the way your company operates?"

Boyd Selden gave him an impatient look. "I've tried to tell you, you just don't understand business."

"That may be," Jim Bannister retorted. "But I think I'm beginning to catch on! The things you've shown me, so far, are right in line with what happened to me in New Mexico. Maybe I couldn't blame these Turkey Ridge men, not wanting to have anything at all to do with you *or* the syndicate!"

Selden stiffened, and Bannister saw him change color. Theirs was a bizarre working relationship, brought about by circumstance, and at the moment it seemed about to break apart in hostility. The syndicate man opened his mouth as though for some angry reply, then clamped it shut again and turned his head away.

They rode awhile in strained silence, Bannister keeping a watch for danger from Selden's enemies. Presently he commented, "I see someone I think we should talk to."

Boyd Selden looked and answered sourly, "I've already talked to him." But he let the other lead the way, dropping down random trails that crisscrossed this ravaged ridge face. They drew rein where a weather-faded tent was pitched beside a timbered adit. It was a typical small workings, rather neater than some. Through the flap of the tent they could see carefully stowed bedroll, supplies, and extra clothing hanging from the ridgepole. Wood was stacked near the tent, an ax with a shining bit leaning against it.

A set of wooden rails led out from the tunnel mouth. Jud Murrow, in jeans and worn boots, a red undershirt and miner's cap, stood beside a mule-drawn ore car with a shovel in one hand as he watched the newcomers approach. He looked at Boyd Selden guardedly, but his nod to Bannister was sociable.

Selden, on the other hand, couldn't keep a supercilious note from his voice as he told Bannister, "You see here the rock bottom of a mining operation—one man and a mule and a shovel! Murrow, when are you going to admit that it takes capital to work a silver claim, even the size of this one?"

The other man seemed unwilling to take offense. He grinned faintly as he told the syndicate man, "I guess somebody like you can't imagine trying to do anything on such a puny scale. But a lot of us are finding good color—traces of galena and gray copper that's paid off for the other workings in this camp. After all, one real vein is all a man needs to hit."

"Like the Teakettle's, I suppose?"

"Why not? That's proof the stuff is here. All the more reason to keep digging."

Jim Bannister asked the syndicate man, "Do you have that note with you?" Selden shrugged as he passed over the paper that had been shoved under his door; Bannister handed it to the miner and watched him read it. "What's your opinion?" he demanded. "Had you heard anything that might indicate something's gone wrong with the Teakettle's big vein?"

Jud Murrow hesitated before answering. "Don't forget," he pointed out, "rumors are what a camp like this one lives on. . . ."

"Then this *isn't* exactly news to you?" Bannister insisted.

"Perhaps you have a notion," Boyd Selden put in, "who might have written that note and had it slid under my door."

"No, I honestly don't, Mister Selden. It could have been nearly anyone, I guess, who had heard the rumor." He handed back the note, and Selden returned it to his pocket.

"Who'd be in a position to know definitely if there was anything in this?"

He had to wait as Murrow thoughtfully rubbed a hand across his jaw. "I couldn't say, unless it would be one of the Teakettle crew. That's a peculiar setup—a handpicked outfit, and mighty close-mouthed about anything that goes on up there. And there ain't much turnover."

"But still," remarked Selden, "the note *might* have been written in an effort to make trouble for Herron or Kimrey, by someone they had occasion to lay off."

"Yes, I guess it's possible. You know, a man that's up to his neck in his own affairs, he don't always hear much of what's going on." Jud Murrow indicated his claim, the impatient mule and the work awaiting him.

Jim Bannister had one last question. "Maybe you heard about a cave-in in one of the Teakettle's tunnels this morning—bad enough to make them close down operations?" Murrow's blank expression answered for him. Bannister went on, "I thought not. If there was any truth in it, that mine would be boiling like an anthill somebody poked with a stick. But nothing's happening up there at all."

"Miles Kimrey is lying," Boyd Selden said flatly, and lifted the reins. He told Bannister in an angry tone, "Let's be going. We've wasted enough time."

Jud Murrow watched them ride away, his weathered face wearing a puzzled frown. Afterward he turned back to his work of emptying the ore car, but rested the shovel again when he saw

Lewt Flagg and another approaching, loose dirt and gravel sliding beneath their boots.

Flagg, he thought, looked dangerous—still carrying a grouch, no doubt, over his besting in the saloon fight last evening. His companion, a lantern-jawed brute named Dill Sheckley, had worked for Flagg and McIver on their claim adjoining the Teakettle mine; now that McIver was dead, there were only Flagg and Sheckley left to work it. Flagg came to a stand in front of Murrow. Without preliminary he said, "That was interesting! Getting kind of thick with that syndicate pair, ain't you?"

Suspicious by nature, Lewt Flagg was bound to misinterpret what he had seen. Murrow shook his head as he answered patiently, "They just stopped by for a word. I talked to them."

"Sure you did," Flagg said heavily, showing his teeth in a smile that suddenly turned ugly. "What the hell would they want to talk to *you* about?"

"Nothing that concerns you."

A heavy fist came over and smashed Murrow in the face, taking him by surprise and sending him stumbling back against the ore car. Blinking, he muttered a protest but Flagg was right after him; a second blow broke the skin above his cheekbone and another sank into his middle, doubling him forward. Flagg straightened him out with a solid jolt against the jaw.

Dazed by the suddenness and the bruising power of big Flagg's fists, Murrow managed now to get his footing and, belatedly, bring his arms up to protect himself; but Flagg had done what he wanted. Menacing the other with his size, he waited to see if Murrow would try to return any of what he had taken. When the latter merely stared at him in bewilderment, the big man wagged his head and stepped back.

"Let that remind you," Lewt Flagg said harshly, "any dealings with the syndicate concerns the whole Ridge! Just one of us giving way, and letting them have the foothold they want—that's absolutely all it would take!"

Murrow put a trembling hand to his cheek, looked at the blood that smeared his fingers. Dill Sheckley stood by, no feeling in his bovine fcatures.

"I don't know why you're getting tough with *me!*" Jed Murrow cried. "I ain't sold out. Nor has anybody else that I've heard of."

"You was talking to them," the big man repeated doggedly. "And now I come to think of it, lately I've been hearing you say some things I ain't liked too much—about scrape together, to develop these Turkey Ridge claims. The syndicate would love to have us believing that!"

Murrow answered, "I got a right to say what I think. Maybe I *am* having some doubts—but long as the majority favors hanging on, I'll go along.

129

At least while I can. You won't see me letting anybody down."

He endured Flagg's black look that seemed to be trying to probe behind his eyes. The big man nodded, making it a menacing gesture. "You better mean that! You damn well better! We ain't going to fool around with traitors. Right now I'd say that slick-talking bastard, Selden, and his hired gun have had all the rope they got coming. The time has come to act."

"That kind of thinking got Ed McIver killed," Murrow warned him. "Be careful you don't make as bad a mistake."

"Just don't get in my way!" Lewt Flagg said, and wheeling away he went tramping off toward his own claim, towing the thick-witted Dill Sheckley in his wake.

CHAPTER XI

Selden and Bannister, dropping back down to the floor of the gulch where the camp lay in midday sunshine, met the carriage and team at the edge of town; black leather and metal trappings glinted, hoofs flashed, the yellow wheels dripped dust. J. T. Herron, with Flora Gentry beside him, nodded pleasantly to the riders and gave the liveried black driver a prod with the end of his silver-headed walking stick. The carriage halted.

The two riders had automatically touched their hat brims to Flora Gentry. She looked at her best, a buxom woman in a well-cut brown suit that set off the darker tints of her hair. From beneath her parasol she regarded Jim Bannister, her red lips unsmiling. Plainly she hadn't forgotten the request he refused her last evening in the hotel parlor.

"Fine morning—fine morning," said Herron, and a red stone on one hand flamed as he made an expansive gesture. "I'm just running up to take a look at the work on my new house. You gents out for a little constitutional?"

"We might as well have been," Boyd Selden told him grimly, "for all the good we did ourselves! We've been up on Turkey Ridge. Perhaps you'll remember, you gave me a standing invitation to inspect the Teakettle."

Herron brushed a hand across his flowing mustache. "That's right," he agreed. "Any time at all."

"As it turned out, your man Kimrey wouldn't let us light; not without a direct order from you, he said. It's something about a mining accident— one of the drift tunnels collapsed. . . ."

"Oh?" If J. T. Herron was in the least concerned, he failed to show it. "Well, naturally, Miles Kimrey is in complete charge up there; I have too many irons in the fire to go poking my nose into his business and getting in the way. I'm sure you see how it is."

"I'm sure I do," Boyd Selden said, in a tone that drew him a hooded look from J. T. Herron's spaniel eyes.

Bannister, watching, saw the look quickly withdrawn. Herron thrust a hand into his coat pocket, brought out a silver case and took a cigar from it. "But if there's anything else I can do for you . . ." he suggested, too casually.

"Not a thing that occurs to me at the moment." Deliberately turning from him, Selden again nodded to the woman. "Ma'am," he murmured, and was gone. Bannister, riding after him, saw Herron's quick scowl and the unreadable, troubled depths in the woman's brown eyes.

He fell in beside the syndicate man and said dryly, "I couldn't see that Herron was too much concerned about a mishap at the Teakettle."

Selden smiled thinly. "He didn't know what excuse his man would rig to keep us out of there, but he knew Kimrey could be relied on. I'm afraid one thing really has him bothered, though."

"Yes?"

"He was counting on me asking for another appointment, to argue his terms some more. Now he's worrying whether he may have let me slip off the hook." Selden, in a bad temper earlier, appeared suddenly to be amused.

But he also showed weariness; from the tightness of his cheeks Bannister realized the man's bullet wound was bothering him. When they made their way through the traffic of the camp and pulled rein in front of the hotel, Selden passed him the reins and swung stiffly down. He was rubbing his arm as he gave orders: "Turn this animal back to the livery for me. And while you're at it, stop by the stage office. Find out what time the westbound coach pulls out tomorrow, and book me on it for San Francisco."

Bannister looked at him. "You're actually leaving?"

"If matters can't be brought to a head by then, I consider I'll have spent as much time here as I can afford to—much as I would hate to go empty handed. But I'm making a little bet: J. T. Herron will undoubtedly get word of this within the hour—and when he thinks he sees me passing up the bait, he'll have to make the move and break our deadlock."

Lifting the reins, Bannister nodded, "Whatever you say."

"While you're there," Selden told him, "buy yourself a ticket. Frisco is a good-sized town, and it's considerably farther away from New Mexico—a place to lose yourself. If you haven't the fare, I'll pay."

For a long moment Bannister studied the other. But he shook his head. "No thanks. I guess not."

"You still don't trust me that well. Is that it?"

"Maybe. Or maybe I'm not quite ready yet to leave Colorado."

"I don't have to tell you it's getting pretty hot for you!" Selden added, "Or are you thinking of the woman in Morgantown?"

Bannister refused to answer. He waited until the other had turned and walked into the hotel; then, leading the rent horse, he set off through busy traffic toward the livery.

Spotting the stage company's sign, he stopped in there to inquire about the westbound stage and learned it was scheduled to make up at eleven in the morning. When he gave Selden's name, he caught the surprised flick of the agent's stare, his brief hesitation before writing it down. He didn't need to be told that Selden had guessed right: In a few minutes, obviously, word would be on its way to J. T. Herron's office.

He turned up the ramp of the Wideawake Livery, and in the musty stillness dismounted while he looked around for the hostler who should have been on duty. There was no sign of him—sneaked out for a drink, most likely; in some irritation Bannister undertook to do the man's chores himself. He started with the rent horse, stripping the gear and saddle from it. Having carried these to the rack, slung the saddle in place and spread the blanket and hung the bridle over the horn, he returned to take care of his dun.

The slur of a boot on loose straw gave him a second's warning. Half turning, he caught a glimpse of the figure moving on him from the shadowy box of a stall; he saw the faint gleam of the upraised gun descending toward his head. He managed to sidestep and the assailant missed, his arm striking the stall's edge and drawing a grunt of pain from him.

But Bannister's quick move had thrown him off balance and the treacherous straw underfoot slid beneath his boots; he fell away and down, to one knee, as he felt for his own gun. Even as it came out into his hand he saw, too late, that there were two attackers. All at once the second one was rushing in, half running over him. A knee slammed painfully into his back. He twisted about, striking out blindly with the barrel of the gun.

Then the weight of a six-shooter landed full against the side of his head. Cushioned only by his hat, it filled his head with a bloom of splintered light and pain. He dropped into nothingness.

There was little sensation of forward movement. At first, something seemed to be pounding him in the face, and for all his muddled efforts he could not manage to turn his head away or lift a hand to defend himself. Then as his head cleared slightly he had the impression of lying facedown on a hard flooring, that shook and tossed him bodily in an irregular rhythm. His arms, he judged, were fastened behind him, so that with each jolt he received he took the shock helplessly on the side of his face that lay against the splintered boards. Dust hung about him chokingly.

He became aware, then, of the creaking of timbers and the grind of ironshod wheels, and the thunderous slam of a springless wagon box under him; slowly it came home to him that he lay trussed and unceremoniously dumped into the bed of a rig that was crawling over the ruts and stones of an uneven roadway. Something lay over him and weighted him down, almost smothering him: a tarpaulin, he decided, flung over him to cover and conceal him so that no one seeing the wagon could guess it contained a helpless captive.

Where the gun barrel had struck the back of his head, a steady, throbbing ache was centered; aggravated by the pounding he was taking from the wagon bed, it seemed enough to lift the top of his skull. In an effort to reduce the punishment, Jim Bannister attempted to roll onto his side. His bound arms prevented it. Falling back, he rested a moment, gathering his strength, and then tried again.

The effort was too much. In the middle of it, as he strained with teeth gritted against the bonds and the weakness that held him, awareness slipped away and he lost consciousness again.

It was a light stabbing at his eyes that roused him.

He slitted his eyes open, squinted them painfully shut again before he realized that the glaring brightness was actually nothing more than the feeble yellow glow of a lantern. He lay on his back, on hard rock, his arms pinioned beneath him and almost without feeling from the pressure of his own weight and from the ropes that bound them.

The lantern pulled back and now he could make out the legs and boots of a dozen men ranged about him. Their faces were undistinguishable in the upwash of light from the lantern held by one of them. Past them he could see nothing at all; but the odd quality of sound, the dead feel of the air, and the faint gleam of the rough rock wall against which he lay, told Jim Bannister that he was in a mine tunnel. He had no recollection at all of being brought here.

As though echoing the question in his own mind, a voice asked, "How'd you manage this, Flagg?"

"It took some doing," Lewt Flagg answered—Bannister made him out now, among the others, "But me and Dill Sheckley got him. We hauled him up in the back of a wagon—under a tarp."

"You're sure nobody saw?"

Flagg snorted angrily. "You think I'm simple? I made damned sure!"

There was silence for a little. Then someone else said, in a troubled tone, "I hope you don't mean to leave him trussed up this way—like an animal. The man's been hurt!"

"Nothing worse than a little knock on the head, to quiet him down," Lewt Flagg said. "And, you're damn right I'm keeping him tied! I don't take chances with mad dogs, and hired killers!"

The one who had first spoken said dubiously, "But just what good has this done? Seems to me it can only make things worse. Do you imagine the syndicate will call it quits, because one of their hirelings happens to disappear?"

"All we need is to make Boyd Selden call it

quits," Flagg corrected him. "Believe me, once let it sink in that he's gone and lost his protection, and that man will turn rabbit. And when *he* runs, that's the last we'll hear of the syndicate."

"If you believe that, Flagg," Jim Bannister said, "then you're an idiot!"

That caused a stir; they hadn't known the prisoner was conscious. Shadows danced and trembled as the one who held the lantern inadvertently jiggled it in his surprise. As they stared at him Bannister struggled up to a half-sitting position, one shoulder propped against the rock wall. The effort set his head to pounding again, and a thousand needles began working at his arms as his weight came off them.

He could make out faces better now; he saw Jud Murrow, and a number of others he recognized— the Turkey Ridge miners, of course. He looked from one to another, and he told them, "For the moment, you may think you have things your own way. You may even go ahead and finish the job your friend McIver tried, and murder Boyd Selden. Just remember the syndicate has plenty of other agents. And if you insist on violence, they can hire an army."

An oath broke from Lewt Flagg; he waded forward a step and a heavy boot swung and caught Bannister below the ear. The prisoner thought his head would burst apart. He braced himself for the next blow, but it never landed.

For somebody spoke Flagg's name in a note of outrage, and there was a brief scuffling as he was dragged back from his enemy. The lantern bobbed wildly. Then, as Bannister's vision settled, he heard Jud Murrow speaking for the first time, "This has already gone too far. You better turn him loose!"

"Sure—you'd like that, wouldn't you?" Flagg retorted, rounding on him. "You still claim you're not fixing to sell us out to the syndicate?"

"No matter how often you say that, it's still a lie!" Murrow told him, with more spirit than one might have expected. Squinting through the pain in his skull, Bannister watched him face the scowling Lewt Flagg. He seemed a little different somehow—one cheek appeared swollen and discolored. Unlikely as it seemed, the mild-mannered Jud Murrow looked almost as though he had been in a fight.

Just now he sounded stubbornly determined. "Flagg," he said, "you know damn well I've kept my mouth shut and gone along with you like all the rest. But what happens if Selden goes to the constable when Bowers fails to show up? What if Tom Slate gets a court order and comes hunting for him—and *finds* him?"

"Slate can hunt," the big man answered, "He won't find him. Hell, you don't think I'm stupid enough to hold him here, in my own tunnel? We only wanted the lot of you to see we really had him on ice. Where we'll be taking him now, ain't anyone gonna lay eyes on him."

"And where's that?"

"Don't worry. I got a place."

Jim Bannister dragged a breath into his lungs. He still felt dizzy from the kick of that heavy cowhide. In a voice that sounded like a croak he said, "You know he'll take me out and kill me!"

He thought Flagg was going to go for him again, but a savage curse was all he got. "You bastard!"

"You talked plenty about killing him," Jud Murrow pointed out to the big leader, "even before he licked you in the saloon last night. You should know by now the rest of us want no part of bloodshed. I'm going to insist you be held strictly accountable for his safety."

There was a quick murmur of agreement from the rest. And Lewt Flagg, seeing them united against him, gave in with poor grace. "All right— all right," he growled. "If the lot of you are that much concerned about saving this murderer's hide, then you can have him. Once Selden's been convinced he ain't to get what he wants, I don't care what you do with the sonofabitch."

Someone remained a shade dubious. "You mean this? We've got your word on it?"

"My word," Flagg answered carelessly. And Jim Bannister, helplessly watching, knew with, a sinking feeling that the others—Jud Murrow, even—accepted this assurance.

They actually believed Lewt Flagg, probably because it was to their interest to believe him. But the prisoner, who understood better the depth of Flagg's hatred and the violence in his nature, felt a dismal certainty that they had merely signed his death warrant.

CHAPTER XII

J. T. Herron never came away from an inspection of his new house without a warm glow and a renewed sense of his own wealth, achievements, and importance. With its round, crenelated turret tower, topped by a pair of fake gargoyles, it represented his idea of a medieval baron's castle from which, in a more romantic place and era, he might once have looked down upon his fiefdom from a crag above the Rhine. The interior was only roughly finished, but the twenty-foot ceilings were in place, and the sweeping staircase whose curve filled much of the big reception hall; he could already imagine the final effect when the turkey-red carpets and the plush window drapes were in place, and the furniture that was being custom-built to his own design.

As he walked out of the chill of the unheated building, into yellow sunshine, his nostrils were full of the rich smells of new paint and lumber and plaster; in his mental notebook he had just jotted down a brand-new thought for the house that excited him: Solid silver doorknobs throughout! Silver was his trademark, and the source of his opulence; what more fitting than to have it under his hand, every time he passed through one of the thick oaken doors? Yes, he must give the orders at once. . . .

Flora Gentry had already seen all she wanted and was waiting in the carriage, parasol tilted against the strike of the sun—sometimes he felt she almost seemed bored with the entire project of the house, an attitude he could in no way understand. Now as he climbed in beside her, almost before he signaled the black driver, she broke into his pleasant thoughts to ask abruptly, "Where are we going from here?"

He blinked. "Why—I dunno. Back to town, I guess. Did you have something in mind?"

Her answer was almost too casual. "After what that man Selden told you, about some kind of trouble at the Teakettle, I would have thought you'd want to find out just what's going on. And, I've never seen this Turkey Ridge I keep hearing so much about."

Scowling, Herron ran a palm down across his mustache. "Ain't nothing up there that'd interest you—just a bunch of fools, going broke on claims they ain't got the capital to develop. As for the Teakettle, I got a good super in charge. No problems that Miles Kimrey can't handle."

"Still," she persisted, "you don't *know* how serious this may be. I can't understand you not wanting to see for yourself."

144

For just a moment he wondered at a possible hidden motive, but her expression was bland enough. Humoring her, he said, "Well—all right, if that's your idea of a pleasure jaunt," and he gave the driver his orders.

Miles Kimrey was standing before the shaft house, scowling at a note one of his men had handed him, when the carriage pulled to a halt. He showed surprise as he came forward, pocketing the paper; his teeth flashed in a smile of greeting. "This *is* unusual!" he murmured, and nodded to the woman. "Mrs. Gentry . . ." Turning back to his boss he wanted to know, "Anything special bring you up here?"

Herron made a gesture with one soft palm. "Just curious how things were going."

"They're good enough," Kimrey said, before Herron's frown and slight shake of the head could warn him. Too late he seemed to catch the hint of puzzlement in the face of Flora Gentry.

J. T. Herron said hastily, "We run into that syndicate fella a while ago. He'd heard something about an accident up here—said it kept you from showing him around the property. I hope it's nothing serious."

"Oh—that." Miles Kimrey had his cue now; they were on safe ground again, after what could have been a serious crossing of signals. "I guess I did lay it on a little, for Selden's benefit. There wasn't all that much damage—still, I didn't have time for some damn greenhorn being underfoot, while the crews were busy with the cleanup."

"Sure," J. T. Herron agreed, giving him a wink which the woman didn't see. "And you were right. Hell, if he got down in there and something happened, the syndicate would sue us for every dime they could screw out of the court. No—you keep him out, Miles, until it's good and convenient. You can tell him those are my orders."

"Right, J. T."

The two exchanged a nod of understanding. And then Herron turned to the woman who had laid a hand upon his arm. "What is it, Flora?"

"I want to go down there," she said.

He blinked. "In the mine?" He knew determination when he saw it, and having never been able to refuse her anything he could only stammer lamely, "But—why?"

"Because I've never been. You've said more than once you'd take me through one of your workings. What's wrong with right now?"

"Well, I—I dunno . . ." he floundered. Miles Kimrey came to his rescue.

"It's hardly a place for a lady, Mrs. Gentry. Certainly not in those clothes you're wearing—they'd be ruined."

"That's right, honey," J. T. Herron put in quickly. "I'll take you down sometime soon—I promise; but you got to come prepared. Anyway, it's time I was getting back to the office. Now, you ain't mad at me?" he added anxiously.

Flora had turned away from him, a pout upon her doll-like face. He sighed, and spoke a word to his driver that got the carriage into motion again, down the steep road from Turkey Ridge. Fidgeting and pulling nervously at the ends of his mustache, J. T. Herron studied the woman who sat beside him.

He had feared his wife, and now he feared his mistress. He was fairly sure she would not have approved his project of unloading a worthless, played-out mine on the syndicate man, Boyd Selden, and so was determined she should never know about it; but suddenly he had to face the unsettling thought that, perhaps, she'd somehow guessed.

It was a good thing that in Miles Kimrey he had someone he could depend on to help keep the secret from her. . . .

Eyes narrowed, Kimrey watched the shiny black-and-yellow carriage roll away behind its saffron veil of dust. No question, that woman had the damn fool under her thumb; it made a situation loaded with dynamite. He remembered then the note he had shoved in his pocket and he took it out and read it over again, gnawing at his lip. Nothing but fools anywhere, he thought disgustedly. Coming to a decision he turned to one of his men. "Saddle up for me and bring the horse around," he ordered.

In the office he got his hat and, on a cautious impulse, pulled open a drawer of the desk and took from it a snub-nosed revolver. Checking the loads, he shoved the gun behind his belt, where the natural fall of his coat front covered it. When he came out of the office and down the steps, a roan gelding was waiting under saddle. Swinging astride, he told the man who handed him the reins, "Look for me back in a couple of hours. . . ."

Leaving Teakettle, he took a little-used and scarcely marked trail that quickly carried him away from the workings that scarred the face of Turkey Ridge. Where the ridge abutted upon a higher and rougher fold of the mountains, the trail threaded a pass and from there he followed it down into a region so remote that it could have been on another planet. He dropped below the invisible line marking off another life zone and was in thick timber for awhile, with only occasionally a glimpse of barren, saw-toothed peaks.

Another of those thunderstorms—almost a daily occurrence here—was beginning to pile up a threatening mass of gray-shot cloud against a cobalt sky. Kimrey reached behind him and, feeling the reassuring stiffness of a slicker strapped behind the saddle, promptly forgot about the weather.

A few more miles brought him across a barren shoulder and to the head of a gulch. In a thin remnant of the forest that had once covered all this region, a closed-down mine workings scarred the barren hill face with the black mouth of its adit, the heaps of waste, the broken and rotting remnants of crude buildings—nature would need considerably longer before it could cover the ugly ruin that greedy men always seemed to leave behind them.

Such a thought was foreign to Miles Kimrey's way of looking at things and it never crossed his mind now. He pulled up in the trees and surveyed the scene during a long couple of minutes, checking for movement and seeing it, finally, in a pole corral half-hidden among the trees; he counted three horses there. He studied the wagon road at the bottom of the gulch, where supplies and ore had once flowed to and from these abandoned workings, but whose twin ruts were now weed-grown and neglected.

Finally satisfied, Kimrey kicked the roan forward out of the trees, approaching the most substantial of the remaining buildings—a reduction shed, long and narrow, that had been built at a slant down the contour of the steep face of the hill.

The rattle of hoofs in broken rock litter carried clearly in this stillness. It brought a man into the open, appearing in a doorway at the lower end of the reduction shed, while another suddenly came springing around the corner of one of the smaller buildings yonder with a gun in his hand. When they recognized the newcomer the first dangerous tension went out of them; Dill Sheckley plowed to a halt, while big Lewt Flagg folded his arms and leaned a shoulder against the frame of the door behind him.

Flagg waited until Kimrey pulled rein, to sit scowling down at him. A gust of wind, out of the cloud bank piling behind the peaks, whipped along the slope and tugged at their clothing; it carried the scent of coming storm.

"I guess you got the word I left for you," Flagg said. "Wasn't any need for you to come rushing out here, though."

"I'm not so sure," the Teakettle manager said. "You could play hell, if you're not careful! Where have you got him?"

Turned quickly surly, Flagg jerked his head toward the door behind him. "In there," he answered gruffly. "But he ain't saying much."

Stepping down, the other dropped his horse's reins and moved past Flagg to pull open the door; yonder, Sheckley appeared satisfied that all was in order and turned away on business of his own, as Flagg let the manager precede him into the sprawling reduction shed.

Flush against the slope, it had been built in tiers, making use of gravity in each step of the process of separating ore and gangue until, here

150

at the bottom level, the concentrates were finally sacked and loaded for shipment. Nearly all the old equipment had been removed when the mine closed down; the windows had been boarded. Now, within these walls which had once throbbed to the pulse and racket of mill machinery, there was only darkness and dust and, imbued into the very timbers, a pungent trace of the smell of chemicals.

Leaving the door open for light, Flagg led the way to where a man lay motionless, bound hand and foot, against the rough plank wall. As Kimrey watched, a look of distaste on his well-groomed features, Flagg seized the prisoner by his clothing and hauled him up so his head flopped over and his face came into the light. He looked in a bad way—his face cut and swollen, yellow hair and shirtfront stiff with his own blood. Bowers hung limp in Flagg's grasp, eyes closed and one of them swollen and livid.

Miles Kimrey said dryly, "Looks like you'd been working him over a bit."

"The bastard was asking for it!"

"And now that you've got him where you want him, I can see he's been getting it!"

Flagg's curt laugh held a gloating amusement. He flung the prisoner away in such a manner that the side of his head struck the wall. Bowers dropped like a half-filled sack. Kimrey grunted, "You damned sure he isn't dead?"

151

"He's tougher than that," Flagg answered with a shrug. "Likely *would* be dead, but those fools I'm dealing with had the nerve to lay down the law to me. So, for the time being I guess I got to keep him alive."

Kimrey frowned, eyeing the motionless shape of the prisoner. "I wonder," he said, "if it's occurred to you it isn't all this easy for a man to disappear, without a trace. After all, there's his horse at the stable in town—his personal belongings in his hotel room. No one's going to believe he'd leave without them."

"You don't give me much credit for brains, do you?" Flagg retorted. "I just came back from taking care of all that. His horse is up in the corral, right now; and I've got his stuff—walked right into the hotel and helped myself to it."

Kimrey eyed him bleakly. "I hope to God you didn't let anyone see you at it—or follow you here!"

"I could say the same thing to you!"

For a moment, as they stared at each other above the unconscious body of the prisoner, a raw hostility sparked between them. And in this moment the rain began.

It came sweeping down the hill, and as it struck the shed it seemed to start at the high upper end and march the whole length of the roof, until they were engulfed in the racket of the downpour. Thunder crashed and rolled; lightning flared outside the open doorway, dimly flickering in the dusty gloom of the shed. Kimrey had to raise his voice, to be sure of making himself heard above the noise:

"I'm still not convinced this will get rid of the syndicate man—I put a lot more confidence in the unsigned note I managed to have slipped under his door last night. I knew that would get his suspicions up; sure enough, this morning he was at the mine trying to have a look inside. Naturally I turned him down, and I managed to look just guilty enough that I'm sure, now, he's as certain as Herron that the property is worthless."

"Then what is there to worry about?"

"We have a new problem," Kimrey answered. "Herron himself. He's been up nosing around the Teakettle—the first time he's so much as set foot on the place since he put me in charge. He had that whore of his with him, and she was all for going into the mine. Herron would have let her if I hadn't done some fast talking."

Flagg swore softly. "What's the Gentry woman's angle?"

"Maybe she hasn't any, but I'm suspicious. Because if she *is* onto something, she'll never let go—not if I know that bitch! She'll be back, dragging J. T. Herron with her: He'd do anything to humor the woman."

Anxiety unsteadied Lewt Flagg. "Hell!" he exclaimed. "You know we don't dare let either

153

one of them into that mine, to get a hint of what we've been up to!"

"I know. And I've decided what I'm going to have to do to prevent it. It should have been done before this."

"And what is it?"

"Blow up Herron's mine for him."

The other man blinked. "You ain't serious!"

"Enough charges, set off in the right places, can seal the shaft and collapse the main tunnels, do so much damage no one's apt to want to sink money into putting it back in operation—especially since I've got both J. T. and the syndicate thinking the big vein on the third level is already lost. It should take off all the pressure, and give us as much time as we need to finish stripping that vein."

Flagg hadn't yet absorbed the enormity of the suggestion. "Ain't there any other way? Something could go wrong!"

"No chance. I've got Mort Pines—the best powderman on the lode. There'll be no foul-up with him handling it."

"Even so, nobody's going to think for a minute it was an accident! They'll know a thing that size had to of been set."

"I thought of that too," Kimrey said patiently. "So, we throw them a red herring. We'll need someone from the opposition, someone to be seen and killed by the night watchman—but too

154

late to prevent him setting the charges. When we produce his body, our story will be taken for granted. Now, can you give me someone like that?"

Understanding, Lewt Flagg's mouth spread slowly in a grin. "Hell, I got just the one! A bastard named Jud Murrow—he's been making nothing but trouble, trying to balk me at every turn. When you want him delivered?"

"Tonight."

"You're going to blow it tonight?"

Miles Kimrey said crisply, "This isn't to be put off we can't afford the delay."

If Flagg had any urge to argue, he swallowed it. "All right, if you say so," he grunted. "I'll carry out my part."

"See that you do!" Kimrey answered, and went out to his waiting horse.

CHAPTER XIII

For minutes after the sound of Kimrey's going was swallowed up in the storm, there was stillness except for the constant battering of rain upon the reduction shed's long roof. Then Lewt Flagg turned back inside and came again to stand over his prisoner.

For Jim Bannister it was a very bad moment; eyes shut, body numb from the bite of the ropes and from the punishment he had taken, he prepared himself to absorb the thud of boot leather driving into him. Instinct told him the last thing he could afford was to give any hint that he had been listening to every word spoken by his enemies.

Abruptly, Flagg swung away and strode out of the building, closing the door behind him. Bannister let his muscles loosen, only now realizing how severely the pain he had taken, and the expectation of more, had punished him. So far at least the fists and boots of Lewt Flagg did not appear to have dealt him real damage, beyond aching muscles and the cuts and swellings that made his face feel that it was ablaze.

He had been in luck. Cuts and bruises would

heal. Under such treatment, Flagg could easily have killed him—as he meant to do before he was finished.

A ridden horse cantered past the shed now, apparently moving off in the same direction Miles Kimrey had taken. That would mean Flagg was gone to carry out his own share in the night's plans, leaving Sheckley in charge of their prisoner; it also gave Jim Bannister time to forget his own predicament for the moment, and consider the puzzle of witnessing two supposed enemies—J. T. Herron's manager and the leader of the Turkey Ridge men—come together in this most unlikely of places.

Well, it was not the first time unscrupulous men had played one group against another. As far as Jim Bannister was concerned, after all, it should make no real difference if J. T. Herron was robbed of a valuable silver vein, or if the Turkey Ridge men let themselves be duped by their own leader, or Boyd Selden and his company turned out as badly fooled as everyone else. What did bother him was the problem of Jud Murrow. He couldn't quite feel indifferent about Murrow, who at least had tried to be fair—the first of the small-claim men to admit Ed McIver could have attempted to murder Selden, the only one to protest Lewt Flagg's capture and treatment of a man they all took to be a syndicate gunhand.

If Murrow were to die, as a result of

antagonizing Flagg, Jim Bannister knew he was at least partly to blame. . . .

Trying to get into a more comfortable position, he hardly noticed when his clothing snagged briefly on something. A moment later the significance of it struck home. He rolled onto his side so that, with his bound hands behind him, he was able to explore and in this way discover, a few inches above the floor, a square-headed nail whose head had not been sunk quite flush with the wall timber. It was a poor tool, but in his extremity it filled him with a tingling excitement.

By squirming and kicking he managed to get around with back to the wall and then somehow work his shoulders up the rough planks until he was in a half-sitting position. This put his fingers just at the level of the nailhead, and, examining it, he found one rough corner that felt as though it might serve. He shoved the rope that bound his wrists under the edge of the nail and jerked sharply—felt it pluck at the fibers like a metal tooth, and tried again.

It seemed hopeless. The hemp was tough and the nailhead blunt, and he could not see that he was making any distance. Still, it was all he had and doggedly he went to work. After a bit he thought he felt one of the fibers tear, and then another; but it could be an endless task at this rate, and time was passing. As suddenly as it had come, the mountain storm rolled away leaving a muffled sound of water dripping from the eaves and through holes in the rotting roof; but the clouds remained, dimming the light that managed to leak in to him so that it was impossible to judge how much of the day remained. Bannister had a suspicion that it was very late. This added to the pressure and the need for haste; he had to discipline himself to patience.

The small but endlessly repeated movement of plucking rope against nail put an ache into his muscles, that became in time a fire he could not ease by shifting position. Still, his efforts were producing results; probing fingertips could detect the ends of strands that had been torn through. The rope that bound his wrists seemed to be down to something like half its original thickness, when a rattling of boots across the rock rubble of the hillside caused him to freeze, listening.

A hand fumbled at the door; it was flung open and Dill Sheckley came in carrying a tin plate with a cup in the center of it. He walked over to the prisoner and looked down at him.

"So you come around, did you?" he grunted. "I figured you would, by this time." He bent and set the plate and cup on the floor. There were beans and a spoon to eat them with, a chunk of bread, steam curling above the coffee in the cup. The aroma struck at Bannister, reminding him that he had not eaten since early morning. "Fixed myself some grub," the man said, "and I brung you a helping if you want it." He slid the gun from his belt holster. "I'll untie your hands, but don't try anything. Lewt would kill me."

Bannister looked at the gun muzzle pointed at his head. He knew his one chance was lost if he let this man see what had happened to the ropes that bound his wrists. He said roughly, "I'm not hungry."

"Oh?" The thick-witted fellow scowled. "You don't think my cookin's fit to eat, maybe? Well, that's all right! Come to think of it, it'd only be a waste of vittles. Lewt Flagg's gonna be taking care of you, directly he gets back!" Sheckley leered at the prisoner in high good humor. He put the gun away and picked up the plate again, saying, "Damned if I leave good food go begging. I'll just set over here and keep you company, while I finish this off."

He carried the plate a little distance away, where he let himself down on an empty crate with a roof prop for his back; Jim Bannister had to listen to him make animal noises as he ate, spooning up beans and guzzling coffee and tearing at the bread. It occurred to Bannister that shadows were thickening, that the light from the open door was feebler now. This gave him warning of how the hours were flying, how little time remained till nightfall.

He had no choice. Even with Sheckley sitting

a few feet away he set to work again, at the rope and nail.

It might be risky, but in the half-light of the shed he hoped the small movements he made were not visible. He kept his eyes on the man as he worked with caution but steady determination, breath coming a trifle shallower now as he felt more and more fibers parting under the stubborn assault of the nailhead.

Sheckley finished eating and laid plate and cup and spoon aside, belching with satisfaction. From his shirt pocket he took a battered cigar, worked a moment putting it into shape and fastening down the tattered casing with spit. He bit off the end and was digging for a match, when the last taut strand holding Bannister's wrists snapped asunder.

It happened so unexpectedly that he was unable to prevent a convulsive movement of his arms as the rope parted. Unluckily, Sheckley just then was looking directly at him. Match lifted to pop the head upon a thumbnail, he let the motion freeze. His head tilted forward; Bannister could feel the suspicious probing of the eyes in the pale oval face. "What the hell are you up to?" the man exclaimed around the cigar in his mouth. And tossing the match aside, he came to his feet. Metal whispered against holster leather as the six-shooter slid into his hand.

Bannister tensed, and as the other walked

toward him his eyes never left the gleam of that naked gun barrel. Wary in every movement, Sheckley came to a stand above the prisoner and reached his left hand to seize Bannister's shoulder and jerk him forward. He had to lean slightly; this lowered the barrel of the gun to within inches of the prisoner's face. And Jim Bannister moved, putting all his effort into this one chance.

Sheckley, slow wits apparently locked into the belief that his prisoner's hands were still secure, was fatally slow to react. He blinked as Bannister's left hand suddenly showed itself, in a chopping movement that knocked the gun aside even as his fingers clamped, hard, over the other man's wrist. That jarred Sheckley, too late, into action. He gave a yell, and tried to pull free but only succeeded in dragging Bannister over against him. They went down together, with Sheckley partially trapped underneath.

A fist struck Bannister a wild blow, glancing off a cheek that was already painfully swollen from Lewt Flagg's mauling. He had not relinquished his grip on the hand that held the gun; now they fought for it, silently and desperately. Sheckley had the strength with which years of labor of single jack and pick had deformed his arms and shoulders. Bannister could not seem to wrest the six-shooter from him. At last, in exasperation, he slammed the back of his fist

162

against the floor—once, twice, and three times; the gun suddenly popped out of the man's fingers and went spinning away somewhere, into the shadows at the farther side of the shed.

Loss of the gun appeared to convert the man into a tiger, with a frenzy that took Bannister by surprise. A wild blow caught him on the side of his head, briefly stunning him and breaking his grasp. He tried to regain it, took a pummeling from the other's boots as Sheckley kicked free; jeans' cloth and boot leather slid under his fingers. In the last instant he caught at something thrust into the top of a boot and when Sheckley scrambled away he was left with it in his hand: the haft of a knife.

Sheckley was already halfway across the shed, scurrying on all fours. Bannister, forgetting for an instant that his ankles were bound, made a lunge after him and went down heavily. Yonder, the man was hunting for his gun. Knowing he had only seconds, Bannister turned his attention to hacking with the knife at the rope that bound his ankles.

The hemp was stubborn, but the knife at least was sharp. He felt the strands rip apart, but haste hindered him and cost him many wasted movements while, all too keenly, he was aware of the panting noises of his enemy, rooting like an animal for the gun that he could not seem to locate. Then with a snort of triumph Sheckley found the thing and pounced upon it—just as the last strand of rope parted beneath a slash of the captured blade.

Bannister surged to his feet, only to stumble, and nearly cry out with the agony of returning circulation. For a moment the two men crouched, facing one another across a little distance in the half-gloom of the shed—one armed with a gun, the other a knife. It was no match. Bannister saw he was cut off from escape through the open doorway; his only chance lay in retreat, deeper into this building that slanted above them with the steep incline of the hill.

His arm shot forward, the knife blade streaked a faint glimmer of light as it drove toward Sheckley's head. As Bannister expected, the man flung himself out of the way in plenty of time, but for the fraction of a second it took the danger out of that gun. Bannister used the chance in turning and running, on numbed legs, toward the crude ladder that mounted to the next higher level of the long reduction shed. He mounted it in a scramble, and as he cleared the top the gun went off behind him. He rolled off the ladder and threw himself flat, his face in thick dust, as a second shot followed. The bullet clanged metallic echoes somewhere, apparently striking an ancient boiler.

Behind him, the other levels of the shed went up the hill in stairsteps, connected by ladders and cluttered with the odds and ends that had been left to rust when the mine closed down and the mill was abandoned. No real escape in that direction, and already his enemy had him pinned. To rise—to move at all—would give the man below him a target he would hardly be able to miss. Bannister lifted his head slightly, looked about him for something that might serve as a weapon. There was nothing, not even a club.

Sheckley's voice came up to him, arrogant with confidence: "All right, Bowers! I'll give you one chance to come down from there. If I climb that ladder, I'll be shooting to kill!"

Perhaps ten seconds passed as he waited for an answer; they seemed ten times as long. Then, in the smothering silence left in the wake of the six-gun's echoes, Bannister heard a scuff of boot leather across the warped floor below, approaching the ladder. Slowly he lifted onto his hands and brought one knee forward, setting himself. If he was going to take a bullet, better to meet it head on and fighting for possession of the gun, than crouching like some cornered animal that waited to be shot.

He could hear the man breathing, and then his voice again, directly below: "All right—if this is how you want it!" A boot was placed on one of the ladder's lower rungs. Cloth scraped on wood as Dill Sheckley began to climb.

A different gun spoke then, without warning,

a single sharp explosion from the doorway at the lower end of the shed. Bannister thought he heard Sheckley's strangled gasp of agony; distinctly came the unchecked fall of a body. Unbelieving, Bannister crept forward for a look at the lifeless sprawl at the foot of the wooden ladder below him. After that he raised his eyes to the open doorway where, silhouetted against the deepening dusk outside, the stunted figure of Clee Dorset stood with a gun smoking in his hand.

CHAPTER XIV

The little outlaw looked at the man he had killed, and nudged him with his toe. "An ugly bastard," he remarked dryly. "I'm some surprised you'd let a thing like that get the better of you."

"I guess you'd have to call it one of my bad days," Bannister said.

Clee Dorset peered at him in the gloom of the shed. "I've seen you look better."

"Nothing that won't heal—nothing broke that I know of." He hoped he wasn't being too optimistic. The untended cuts on his face felt like fire, and the soreness from the battering his body had taken was so deep he had narrowly kept from groaning aloud as he made his painful way down the ladder. But, shaky as he was, he could maneuver, and he accepted that as a good token. He said, "The thing I don't understand is how in the world you happened to show up."

Calmly replacing the shell he had spent, the other answered as though the matter were one of no particular interest. "You know how it is, sitting all day at a poker table—a man sooner or later picks up any gossip that happens to be going around. So, today I heard that Boyd Selden's

167

bodyguard was missing, and nobody could decide whether you'd pulled up stakes or had some kind of dirty work done to you.

"It was none of my particular business; you could label it curiosity. I had a hunch Turkey Ridge would be the place to turn up a clue. I went up there and prowled around, not making myself conspicuous, and I saw Herron's manager, Kimrey, come riding in off some back trail that didn't appear to lead anywhere. Half an hour later, while I was still watching, that fellow Flagg that you licked in the Golconda last night showed up on the same trail. Since that didn't make any sense to me, I decided to do a little backtracking and try to find out where they'd been."

"Lucky for me you found it," Bannister said. "And just when you did!"

He leaned—his head pounding—and picked up Sheckley's gun; it was the same caliber as the shells in his own belt, so he holstered it. Stuck in a timber where he had hurled it was the faint gleam of the blade from the dead man's boot; Bannister moved over and pulled it free, and used it to hack through the ropes that still encircled his wrists. Clee Dorset, watching, said in an aggravated tone, "You could at least say what the hell has been going on!"

As he worked with the knife, Bannister explained briefly. "It's one of those things where everybody gets played for a sucker. Kimrey uncovered a big vein of silver down on the third level of the Teakettle, and saw a way to keep it for himself. Herron never bothered to inspect any of the properties he owned, and the crew was handpicked by Kimrey and could be counted on to keep their mouths shut; so he took the risk of reporting that the vein had petered out in country rock, and then made a deal with Flagg and McIver—who owned the claim adjoining— to run a lateral from their own workings and strip the vein, and split the take between them.

"But then Boyd Selden showed up; and Herron, having been convinced the Teakettle was a lemon, got interested in unloading. Kimrey and Flagg had to stop that, any way they could. Ed McIver tried to do it with a rifle, and failed. Lewt Flagg had better luck working up the other Turkey Ridge miners as a buffer against the syndicate. And Miles Kimrey managed to leak the news to Selden that J. T. Herron was trying to sell him a mine he thought was worthless."

Clee Dorset asked, "So what happens now?"

Before answering, Bannister walked to the door and looked out at the tail end of the day. A sorrel horse waited near the shed, grounded by trailing reins, where the little gunman had left it. The clouds were breaking and the wet world had a last faint sheen; but it was fading fast even as he looked at it, and in these mountains the twilight would be short.

Rubbing his wrists, raw from the hemp that had bound them, he said, "What happens now— tonight—is that they figure to close the Teakettle down with dynamite, and bury the evidence for good. They'll leave the body of one of those Turkey Ridge men to explain the dynamiting, and keep anyone from asking too many questions."

"Sounds like somebody's finally using his head."

"Unless they're stopped," Bannister said, in a tone that made the other look at him.

"And who's to do that—you?" The little man shook his head with a pained expression. "Why should you be a hero, to the benefit of the syndicate and J. T. Herron? You'll be no hero—just a damned fool."

"Probably," Bannister conceded. "But it isn't Herron or the syndicate that worries me. The man that's been picked for killing—a man named Murrow—deserves better than that. I figure I owe him something."

"Well, count me out! I've done my good deed for today. I'm not getting mixed up in any more of other people's fights right now."

Bannister said, "Nobody's suggesting it: I thank you for what you did. Someday I'll try to return the favor."

"The rate you're going, you won't live long enough!" the other man retorted and walked out to his waiting horse. He gathered the reins, toed

170

the stirrup that was hardly longer than a jockey's, and lifted himself into the saddle; he looked very high off the ground there. He walked the sorrel over for a final word.

"I'm leaving this country tonight. After I kill a man, wherever I am I get a little fidgety. Something I haven't told you yet, might get you feeling the same way: that marshal, or town constable or whatever he calls himself—"

"Tom Slate," the tall man supplied, and Dorset nodded shortly.

"Slate doesn't know me, and he had no idea I was listening when he walked past my table this morning, talking to some other gent. All I heard was a name, but that was spoke plain enough. The name he said was 'Bannister'. . . ."

The tall man was unable to hide the start that went through him; he saw it mocked by the outlaw's bitter smile. "So, maybe you been around here too long, yourself! You've given that lawman just a little too much time to notice you, and maybe start remembering where he heard about a man that answers to your description. Now—do you still say you're going back?"

Jim Bannister said heavily, "I've got to!"

"Then you *are* a fool!" Clee Dorset retorted, and rode away.

After he had gone from sight, Bannister remained rooted for long minutes, gnawed by a worry implanted by that parting shot. But as he had told Dorset, he really saw that he had no choice; he broke free with an angry movement of his shoulders, and turned away. He thought for a moment of Dill Sheckley's body stiffening on the floor of the shed, but decided best to leave it where it was. He closed the door carefully to keep scavengers out, securing the hasp with a bent nail supplied for the purpose. Then, with a growing consciousness of the passage of time, he made his way across the rubble of the hillside where shadows were already blanketing the fading daylight.

Once he stumbled, went down on one knee and stayed that way a moment, breathing hard. He had taken punishment and his body felt it; it protested at the aching, dizzying weakness and didn't want to get back to its feet and go on. But he toiled ahead across the rubbled slant, and when he reached a clapboard shack that, except for the shed, was the only remaining building more or less intact, he leaned a hand against the rough logs, resting. After that he looked for a door and entered a low-roofed room that smelled of mice and decay; the door, sagging on one leather hinge, scraped as he pushed it open.

There was a rickety table and a couple of stools made of sawed log sections, a packing box nailed to the wall for a cupboard and, in one corner, a rusted iron stove. Smell of scorched beans and boiled coffee took him over there, to investigate the blackened pots sitting on it. There were not enough beans left to bother with, but when he hefted the big iron coffeepot he found it nearly half-full. There were tin cups on a shelf; he filled one, and greedily drank.

The stuff was lukewarm and bitter, but it was what he needed. He emptied it twice, and was left with an awareness of how hungry he was. He rummaged the shelves of the cupboard, found an unopened can of tomatoes and half a loaf of bread. Conscious of the passage of time he sawed the can open with Sheckley's knife and wolfed the tomatoes, tearing off chunks of bread and washing both down with more of the vile coffee.

On one of the shelves he had run across his own six-shooter and he was glad to trade Sheckley's rubber-butted weapon for it. He even found his hat, that he must have lost during the skirmish in the livery stable and that someone had picked up and brought along and flung into a corner. He drew it on gingerly, favoring his aching skull, and went out into the grainy dusk to look for the corral he had glimpsed earlier among some trees.

His dun was there, and an ugly-looking bay that must have belonged to Sheckley. Bannister's saddle and gear were racked on the corral's top pole; he saw at a glance that his roll had been ransacked and then clumsily put together again, but aside from having been rained on it seemed intact. He dropped the poles on one side of the

173

pen, chased the bay horse out of it, and then put the gear on the dun—by the time he finished, the last light was hardly more than a memory and he was working by feel and by the kinesthetic sense of long familiar movements. He drew the cinch tight, pulled himself into the saddle—every muscle protesting—and rode past the reduction shed toward the dim trail that he hoped would lead him back to Silver Hill.

Night deepened as he rode, but the clouds had largely scattered and there was the moon, still full, to aid him. Once he came to a spring, its runneling a musical sound in the night, and got down for a drink. He removed his hat and scooped up handfuls of the cold water to douse his face and head, the shock of it helping to clear his thinking. Having given the dun time to drink, he mounted again and pressed on.

He still had no inkling of a plan in mind.

Lewt Flagg hunkered in the brush, fairly sure that he could not be seen, but able to make out with fair distinction what was going on at the fire near the mouth of the adit, a dozen yards downslope from him. The ground under him held yet a little of the day's warmth but it was cooling out rapidly; the night wind, strengthening, blew along the slope and whipped at the campfire, causing the shadows of the three who stood about it to writhe upon nearby tent canvas.

Flagg ground his jaws in impatience and a stick he had been twisting nervously snapped suddenly between his big hands, like the report of a pistol shot. He froze, thinking it must surely have carried to those about the fire; but the wind and the crackle of the flames must have covered it. They talked on, the sound of their earnest discussion reaching him at odd moments, but not clearly enough for him to make out anything they said. He clenched his empty hands and pressed them against his thighs, swearing silently.

But now one of the men came to his feet, and as the others imitated him their raised voices had a finality that indicated the talk was over. Someone said, "Looks like a clear night," and another answered, "See you boys tomorrow then." A few last exchanges and after that they broke up, two moving off together and a third alone, following the paths that crisscrossed the ridge in a crazy pattern. The one who remained, having called a last good night, stood tamping the bowl of a pipe against his palm; embers from the pipe caught the wind and streamed away, a brief skirl of sparks.

Jud Murrow turned then, as he heard Flagg coming in on his claim. Firelight glinted against his eyes, giving him a startled look that did not entirely disappear when he recognized his visitor. "Flagg?" he exclaimed nervously. "I didn't hear you. Too bad you didn't get here a couple minutes earlier."

"Why? Who's that you were talking to?"

"Willis and Iselin and Perrigo." Murrow named three of the Turkey Ridge miners. "We were jawboning over the way things have been going."

Flagg couldn't quite keep the contempt out of his voice. "And I suppose the bunch of you came to some momentous decision. Something you mean for me to know?"

"We all think," Murrow said bluntly, "that this thing is getting out of hand. We can't make open war on the syndicate. We want Bowers turned loose before something happens that we'll all be sorry for."

Lewt Flagg sucked at a tooth, peering thoughtfully at the other man. "You've decided that, have you? And just who do you think you're speaking for?"

"We hope to bring everyone around to our way of thinking."

"Go ahead!" Flagg told him gruffly. "But right now, Bowers is in a safe place and he's going to stay there. And meanwhile there's something I want to show you."

Murrow showed his puzzled surprise. "Me?" he echoed. He looked around. "What?"

"You'll have to take a little walk over to my claim to see it."

The puzzlement became edged with a first beginning of suspicion. "I dunno, Flagg," Jud Murrow said, and shook his head. "I just don't figure you out. There's something mighty funny about the way you—" The words broke off, the man's body stiffening as Flagg's gun rammed him.

"I ain't fooling with you!" Lewt Flagg told him, letting all the cold hatred flood into his voice. "You done nothing but cross me, and now, by God, you're taking up time I can't afford to waste. Now, stand hitched!" And as the other man held himself tensely still, Flagg frisked his clothing but found no weapon. He grunted and stepped back a pace, letting Murrow see the shine of firelight on the gun barrel pointed at his belly. "All right!" Flagg said. "We're taking a little stroll over to my claim, like I said. And you're going without making me any trouble."

Murrow must have read something in his face that warned him not to defy the gun. Flagg saw resignation come into the line of his shoulders. Murrow seemed to grow a trifle smaller. He dropped the pipe that he still held into a pocket of his windbreaker, glanced uneasily at the fire but apparently decided it would soon die back from lack of fuel and was safe to leave. Without a word he turned and Flagg fell into step beside him, six-shooter in hand. They took a path that would lead directly to the Flagg and McIver workings.

The moon was up, in a sea of stars and broken clouds, and the spreading glow softened some of the ugliness of Turkey Ridge. A host of campfires

177

spotted the face of it, and lamps and lanterns gleamed behind canvas and in the doorways of brush hovels and clapboard shacks. There was a muted quiet along the Ridge after the day's passing. Voices carried, the barking of a dog, somewhere the doleful wail of a harmonica— some men in their ambition and greed might toil at their claims around the clock, working by lanternlight until they dropped, in their frantic search for money rock; but in the end one learned patience and respect for the needs of his body, or he didn't last long.

They passed a few yards upslope of a fire and someone, thinking he recognized Jud Murrow, hailed them. "Wave to him," Flagg ordered tersely, "but don't answer."

Murrow lifted an arm, which would have been visible in the moonlight, and let it fall again; they kept on without slowing pace and the fire was left behind. "You were smart that time," Flagg said gruffly.

"You going to tell me," Jud Murrow demanded in a tight voice, "just where the hell I'm headed? The same place where you're holding Jim Bowers, I suppose?"

Flagg thought that over, and something he found in it split his mouth into a grin. "I guess, at that, you could say you're going to end up the same place."

"You mean, we're both going to be dead!"

Lewt Flagg only laughed, letting the laugh answer for him. A moment later they were in sight of his own claim, with its adit and dump and its shanty—hardly bigger than a packing case—where he and McIver and Sheckley had bunked in crowded squalor. When Murrow started to turn in that direction Flagg grunted and shoved him on with the gun muzzle. They began to climb.

A spread of buildings came in sight, near the top of the ridge. The prisoner halted in mid-stride and turned to exclaim, "That's the Teakettle! What are we going there for?" And Flagg was unable to resist the wicked impulse to tell him as much as he thought Murrow needed to know.

As he talked he heard the breath break from the other man's lips, almost as though he had been slugged above the belt. Murrow said hoarsely, "Are you serious? How could anybody do a thing like this?"

Flagg grinned. "If you could have seen the smelter figures on the silver ore we been taking out these last couple months, maybe you wouldn't have to ask!" He gave the prisoner a shove that sent him stumbling forward. Since the Teakettle did not employ a night shift, the mine layout they were approaching looked shut down and deserted, hardly any lights showing.

Suddenly ahead and a little to the left a voice called sharply, "Murrow! *Drop!*" and was followed by the flat crack of a gunshot—smear of

179

muzzle flame and streak of purple sparks. The shot must have been aimed purposely high, over Flagg's head; but it paralyzed his nerves momentarily and he was unable to respond as Jud Murrow, heeding the shout, instantly flung himself prone.

Flagg let him go. He thought now he caught the shape of a man rising above the dark earth. He looked very big and when he spoke, Flagg was incredulously sure he knew the voice: "You've got a choice, Flagg. Throw away the gun, or use it."

"Bowers!" The name burst from him. Swearing, he threw his own gun around and flung a shot toward the voice. It was answered by a second blast from that other gun, that missed. Suddenly Lewt Flagg found himself running forward, to close with the man he hated. He shot again, blindly; thumbed the hammer back for a third try, without breaking stride.

Then the blaze of the other weapon, almost in his face, filled his vision and seemed to blind him. Something struck him in the chest, massively; pain blossomed from that one tiny piece of lead and seemed to rush outward, spreading through him in every direction. He yelled with the agony of it. And then he was on his knees and his head fell forward, and Lewt Flagg felt nothing at all.

CHAPTER XV

Jud Murrow came to join Bannister as the latter straightened from a hasty look at the man he had shot. "Dead?" The tall man only nodded; apparently the moonlight was bright enough to make out the gesture, for the question wasn't repeated. Murrow looked at the body sprawled in front of them. His voice was shaky as he said hoarsely, "I'd have laid odds it was going to be me instead!"

"It was meant to be you," Bannister agreed. "The way they had it planned, neither one of us was to outlive the night. But it looks like we've still got luck working for us."

"I don't know how you managed—how you got away from them, or turned up here when it counted. And 'thanks' is a lame word."

Bannister shrugged. "I had a few things to thank *you* for," he said, in a tone that closed the subject. He had finished reloading the gun, and with a grimace he holstered it.

Quiet had returned; the sound of shooting must have carried, but there was no sign that it had caused alarm—perhaps gunplay was too common a thing along the Ridge; since it was over so soon, each man who heard it would have decided it was none of his business and best left so. But up at the Teakettle, movement drew Bannister's attention. A man had emerged from the shaft house and was prowling back and forth. A lantern on a pole behind him gleamed from the barrel of a weapon—a shotgun, most likely. The guard appeared to be trying to make out the meaning of the shots that had alarmed him.

Jud Murrow said grimly, "That's a nervous man up there. Not hard to understand, considering what's afoot at the Teakettle tonight!"

"You know about that?"

"Flagg told me—it seemed to give him a lot of pleasure. The funny part of it is, some of the others might have been ready to use dynamite if it would keep the syndicate off the Ridge. But from the very beginning, I've been one who argued against violence."

"That's why you were chosen." Bannister said. "You've been a thorn in Lewt Flagg's side."

"But this thing has got to be stopped!"

Bannister said bluntly, "My guess is that it's already too late. Kimrey's had plenty of time. He could be finished by now and ready to light his fuses."

"I suppose you're right. But to *know*, and just stand by . . ."

The man's concern puzzled Bannister. "Nothing for you to worry about. I'm not aware that you owe J. T. Herron anything."

"That's not the point. I don't like to see some-body like Miles Kimrey go unpunished. Espe-cially now that Flagg is dead, once he puts the Teakettle out of operation he'll have buried all the evidence against him. He'll pocket his share of the loot from stripping that stolen vein, and no way ever to prove it on him. And that don't sit right with me. By God, it don't!" Jud Murrow exclaimed, with a fierceness that seemed odd in such a mild-mannered person. And he knelt, and when he straightened again Bannister saw he was holding the gun Lewt Flagg had dropped.

Bannister exclaimed sharply, "What are you thinking?"

"I'm thinking there's nobody on guard up there—only the one at the shaft house, operating the lift machinery. He shouldn't be too hard to handle."

"And after that?"

"Why, I suppose then it's a matter of taking one step at a time. . . ."

Jim Bannister ran a hand across his face, wincing as he touched the bruised and swollen flesh. He felt soreness in every muscle of his body, a bone-deep lethargy. Until now he'd allowed himself to think no further than the task of somehow saving Jud Murrow; with that done, a host of other matters came crowding in on him: Miles Kimrey and J. T. Herron and the syndi-cate, and above all, the warning he'd had that his identity was known to Constable Tom Slate. If that happened to be true, it made this camp the most dangerous spot in the world for him just now.

But Jud Murrow's honest anger had a contagion about it. Almost in surprise he heard himself saying, "You're right. The guard shouldn't present too much of a problem . . ."

The man had withdrawn into the shaft house, but he was on the alert. When he heard someone approaching, the lantern winked out and next moment he showed indistinctly in the doorway, the shotgun ready in his hands. His voice was edged with tension as he demanded, "Who's out there?"

Bannister halted, just beyond effective reach of the weapon trained at his chest. "I've got a message. For Kimrey."

"He ain't here."

Drawing a breath, Bannister said, "We both know better than that. This is important—it's from Flagg. . . ."

The guard considered. Moonlight gleamed vaguely on the shotgun's barrel but the man himself was only the dimmest of targets. Bannister swore mentally. *Will he ever move out of that doorway?*

"You stand where you are," the man said, and emerged into the moonlight for a better view. Jim

Bannister thought he looked like one of the men who had been here this morning, to watch him ride up with Boyd Selden. If so, Bannister's size could be enough to identify him.

The man halted suddenly; he stiffened and the shotgun moved in his hands. "Wait a minute!" he exclaimed. "Ain't you—?"

And then as Bannister braced himself, ready to roll under the shotgun's blast if he had to, Jud Murrow's voice came from the darkness beyond the guard: "Whatever you're thinking—forget it! Don't move at all. . . ."

Bannister didn't like to admit the relief he felt, as he stepped to take the shotgun from the guard's unresisting fingers and toss it aside. He made a hasty search but found no other weapon. By now Murrow had joined them. Jerking the prisoner about, Bannister hustled him back inside the darkened shaft house.

Badly frightened, the guard tried to stammer something but Bannister had no time to listen. Not liking what he had to do, he drew his gun and as they crossed the threshold he gave the prisoner a clip with the barrel of it, across the back of his neck where it joined the skull. The man jerked and collapsed without a sound. Bannister caught him as he sagged to the floor and then, working by such moonlight as fell through the doorway, hauled the man with heels dragging to drop him out of sight behind the silent donkey engine.

There was no time to tie the prisoner, but he seemed to be out cold and should stay that way awhile. He had been hit pretty hard.

As Bannister straightened something was shoved into his hand and Jud Murrow said, "Put this on." It was a miner's cap; Murrow had also located one for himself. He got both sputtering carbide lamps lighted and showed how they were adjusted. Afterward he said, "They've taken the lift below with them. The guard was waiting for their signal to start the engine and haul them up again."

"How do we go down?" Bannister asked.

"The ladder."

It descended one side of the shaft that opened blackly before their feet. Looking at it, Bannister had a queasy sense of misgiving and was aware of a trace of cold sweat starting inside his shirt. Once, exploring a cave when he was fifteen and growing faster than he realized, he had found himself trapped, stuck fast and helpless in the black bowels of the earth for hours, until rescue came. The boyhood experience had left its scars in a dread of confinement in dark and narrow places. Now the idea of crawling down that flimsy-looking ladder into black nothingness brought up all the buried memories. . . .

He swallowed and nodded. "Whatever you say."

Murrow had shoved Lewt Flagg's six-shooter

behind his belt. Without further words he stepped onto the ladder and began the descent, and Bannister, having let him get a start, gingerly followed.

He had an irrational feeling that the shaft must be without a bottom. The sounds Jud Murrow made, preceding him down into the formless dark, were reassuring. Bannister gripped each rung tightly as his boot groped to find the next. He started to count them but quickly left off. Then, after what seemed an endless time, the other's voice came up to him: "Watch it. Here's the lift. . . ."

Moments later he stepped from the ladder onto a crude wooden platform that swayed slightly on its cables. Murrow was waiting for him. Here, a tunnel extended into the living rock, lighted by a flare burning in a wall socket. Bannister could sense the stillness—like a pressure against his ears. Smoke from the burning torch drifted on the upward draft of a ventilation shaft somewhere, but to him the air felt dead. He met Jud Murrow's stare, and wondered if he showed the queasiness that was bothering him.

Bannister asked, "Would this happen to be the third level?"

"You guessed it. This is where Kimrey found the big vein and then pretended to lose it. Now he's down here making damn sure it really gets lost, for good."

"I hope your sense of direction is working. I think I lost mine."

Murrow peered along the drift that stretched ahead of them. "We're facing east. That puts the Flagg and McIver claim to our left. The vein would lie that way."

"I'll have to take your word for it."

Murrow was holding the gun he had taken from Lewt Flagg's body—holding it, Bannister noted, like a man unused to handling weapons. They started cautiously along the gallery, walking between the rails for the ore cars. The sound of their steps echoed strangely in this dead air; the roof was so low that Bannister had to keep his head bent to clear it.

Presently the feeble glare of their lamps showed a lateral intersecting the main tunnel and they turned into it, bearing left in the hope that this drift would lead to the stolen vein. Jud Murrow said, "Some of these deep mines are cut up in a regular maze of tunnels; but I don't think this one could have been in operation that long." Bannister hoped he was right. Otherwise they could still be wandering down here, trapped but unaware, after Kimrey had set and touched off his charges, and left.

He said nothing. But moments later he suddenly caught at his companion's arm, halting him. Murrow let out his breath when the unmistakable sound of hurrying footsteps came from somewhere ahead—two men, Bannister thought, approaching almost at a run.

"Kill the lamps!" he exclaimed hoarsely.

As total blackness rushed in upon them, it was to Bannister as though the narrow walls closed in with all the weight of the tons of rock that pressed above his head. The atavistic fear of living burial turned his mouth dry and constricted his breathing. Gun in hand, he waited.

Then a bobbing glimmer showed faintly, resolved itself into a glow surrounding the pair of men who approached along the gallery. One wore a miner's cap, the lamp lighted; he had a wooden box under one arm, a coil of fuse looped about his shoulder. The second man, who carried a burning lantern, was Miles Kimrey.

In their hurry they seemed unaware of any presence in this dark tunnel besides their own; but at some little distance the gleam of lamp or lantern must have picked out a warning shape. They halted, and one let out a startled exclamation.

Jim Bannister spoke quick warning: "There are guns covering you both."

The scene froze, for a long count of three, while the Teakettle men absorbed their surprise. Then Kimrey came on a half-step, his head shot forward, the lantern in his hand lifting slightly as though he were trying for a better look. *"Bowers?"* The name exploded from his lips.

And without waiting for an answer he flung the lantern.

He aimed it straight at Bannister's head, a dazzling streak that seemed to swell in size as it came. Bannister blinked and managed to stumble away, feeling the lantern's heat against his face. It struck the wall of the tunnel, missing him by inches, and smashed with a splatter of burning oil. In the same instant, or very nearly, the first gunshot thundered.

His vision already seared by the glare of the exploding lantern, Bannister heard the shot as a thunderous explosion which, in that confined space, seemed enough to burst a man's ears and turn his brain to mush. His shoulder struck the wall, and with that to steady him he leveled his own gun and fired past the dripping smear of burning oil, aiming at the afterimage of muzzle flash. He pulled back the hammer and fired a second time, and a third.

In such close quarters, it was hard to see how any shot could fail to tally. It sounded like a tremendous barrage, each fresh explosion mingling monstrously to shock the eardrums. Yet Bannister felt no touch of a bullet; and as he prepared to fire again he saw, in the dim light of burning oil, the solid shape of Miles Kimrey starting to double forward at the waist. The man fell with a peculiar effect of slow motion. He struck the rock floor of the tunnel, on his face;

and only then did Bannister become aware that the deafening pulse of sound was already fading, and that he and Kimrey alone had been doing all the shooting. As quickly as it had begun, it was over.

His whole head rang with concussion; he found himself fighting to breathe despite the fumes of cordite and burning oil. "Murrow?" he said sharply. "You all right?"

"I—think so!" The man sounded shaken and dazed.

"Take a look at Kimrey," Bannister directed, and turned his attention—and his gun—to the other Teakettle man.

The latter had not moved; he still clutched his box and coil of fuse, and he said now, hastily, "I ain't in this! I got no gun! You can search me!"

"Don't worry—I will!" Bannister promised. "You'd better hold still while I do it."

"You done for Kimrey," Jud Murrow announced in a shaken voice. "You got him dead center!"

There was no answer for that, and Bannister proceeded with his search of the prisoner, finding nothing in the way of a weapon. Obviously he was a powderman, not a fighter. Without protest he handed over the coil of fuse and the box; Bannister guessed the latter's contents before his probing fingers felt the oddly greasy touch of dynamite sticks, nested in sawdust. Shuddering a little, he put the box aside—he'd had little

191

experience with the stuff, and completely mis-
trusted it. In a pocket of the prisoner's jumper
he found a half-empty box of blasting caps, and
appropriated these as well.

"I think your name is Pines," he said.

Mort Pines merely nodded, eyeing the gun that
was aimed at him. By the flicker of burning oil
his face showed a sickly pallor.

Bannister told him, "We don't have to ask what
you and your boss were up to. We already know."

"You got no business down here," the prisoner
retorted sulkily.

His weak anger lacked conviction. Ignoring it,
Bannister said, "If you and Kimrey used up all
the sticks that are missing out of that box, you
must really have done a job!"

Jud Murrow put in, "It's my guess they'd go
through first and get all their charges set, and
primed with fuses of different lengths. Then, if
we hadn't prevented them, they'd have gone
back through and touched off the fuses, and—"
His expression changed. "Good God! You don't
suppose—?"

"They weren't wasting any time when they
ran into us. Looks to me some of the fuses are
already lit. Only our friend here can tell us for
sure."

Feeling their eyes on him the prisoner worked
up a sneer. "Now, that's something for you to
worry about, ain't it?"

"Damn it, we better get out of here!" Murrow cried.

But Jim Bannister, his stare holding the prisoner, held firm. "No." He slowly shook his head. "First we look for those charges and disarm them. We'll take our friend with us while we do it. You *would* like to come along, wouldn't you, Pines? To make sure we don't miss any?"

The man's expression changed as his nerve broke. With a shout of, "Let me go!" he tried to break free; Bannister seized him and flung him back. Crouched against the tunnel wall, frenzied eyes peered from a face shining with sudden perspiration. "Don't you understand? Those damn sticks are on ten minute fuses!"

"Then it doesn't give us much time, does it?" Jim Bannister said coldly. "So you'd better quit stalling. If we blow up before we find them all— you go with us. That's a promise!"

"You *mean* it!" the man whispered through his teeth. "You bastard, you really mean it!" He lurched away from the wall. "Come on then, damn you! *Hurry!*"

And Jim Bannister, knowing he had won his bluff, could only hope his knees still had stiffness left in them. . . .

CHAPTER XVI

Tom Slate, the Silver Hill constable, shuffled papers on his desk and scowled at the pair who stood before him. A stick snapped in the belly of the iron stove, that kept the chill of the mountain darkness out of the jail office. Slate said heavily, "I'm damned if this ain't the wildest yarn I ever listened to! If you didn't agree with each other, in every particular—"

"You've got more than our word, Constable," said Jud Murrow. "Go up to the Teakettle and look at the evidence. And you haven't talked to the prisoners we brought you—the guard, and that fellow Pines. They're ready and anxious to tell everything they know about what Flagg and Kimrey were up to."

Slate ran a palm across his scalp. "I'd like it better if I could talk to Flagg and Kimrey. But you fixed it so I can't do *that!* Not with them both at the undertaker's, getting colder by the minute!" His black eyes sought Bannister's, settling on him with sour frustration.

The tall man returned his stare. "There's still another one, a man by the name of Sheckley, lying dead in an abandoned reduction mill

194

somewhere east and north of the camp. From my description, Murrow says it would be the old Mogul operation."

"I know the place," Slate said impatiently. "But I ain't got it clear yet, how you could have managed to get away from those you say were holding you there."

Jim Bannister hesitated. He had not mentioned Clee Dorset and he preferred to keep the outlaw out of this. He said simply, "I had some luck— and the others were careless."

The constable merely grunted. Boyd Selden, seated by the desk, said critically, "You look in poor shape to me, Bowers. You really ought to see the doctor."

The tall man shrugged. "Lewt Flagg worked me over a bit, while he had me tied up and helpless. I expect I'll mend." He touched the eye that was swollen nearly shut. He was desperately weary, but his physical hurts were of secondary importance to him now as he watched the constable's dark, bulldog face.

Slate chewed at the inside of his lower lip; in the silence, the raucous voice of the silver camp reached distinctly into this room. Finally the lawman moved his heavy shoulders. "Fantastic as it all sounds, I guess I have to believe it. I'll need statements from you both—tomorrow will be time enough."

"All right," Jud Murrow said; and Bannister

nodded, not quite trusting himself to speak.

Boyd Selden, who had been in conversation with the constable when these two brought in their prisoners, rose now from his chair. "It's been a long day," he said. "Bowers, I'll want to see you at the hotel." Bannister nodded shortly.

Selden had opened the door when Jud Murrow spoke suddenly. "Can I talk to you a minute, Mr. Selden?" Hand on the knob, the syndicate man gave him a probing look before nodding curtly; Murrow followed him out, and Jim Bannister was left alone with the constable.

Something in Slate's brooding stare held Bannister. Deliberately he faced the man who was still seated behind the flat-topped desk. His words came out almost as a challenge:

"You want something more from me?"

Slate took his time answering. When he did, it was to ask a question. "Just how long you been working for Selden?"

It sounded to Bannister like a trap, and he parried it. "How long did *he* tell you?"

"Why—don't *you* know?" the other said suspiciously.

"A job's a job; I couldn't say how long I've held this one. Might have been three years, might have been a little longer."

"Or, less? A whole lot less, maybe?" suggested Slate, too quietly.

Backed into a corner, Bannister had to make

a stand. "No," he lied firmly, shaking his head. "Three years at the very least. I'm sure of that." And from the change in the man's expression, he knew he had said the right thing.

Tom Slate scowled, and swore. "That agrees with Selden, all right. But, by God, you could have fooled *me!*" He jerked open a desk drawer, drew out a stiff square of cardboard and tossed it down in front of the other. "Ever seen one of these, Bowers? I swear, the man could be your twin!"

His face carefully under control, Bannister picked up the reward notice. He had seen other copies. The name in block letters was his own, the description accurate, the astounding amount of the reward—twelve thousand dollars—enough to arouse the avarice in any man. But by some stroke of luck the pen and ink sketch was only a passable likeness, resembling him, but just enough unlike to raise a doubt; nevertheless his cheeks felt cold as he looked at it, with a forced indifference.

He managed a half-smile as he lifted his eyes to the lawman. "Yes, it's getting to be an old story. So, you thought I was this what's-his-name— Bannister? And me working for the very outfit that wants his head!"

Slate ran a palm across his heavy jowls, and across the back of his neck. "From the minute I laid eyes on you," he said heavily, "I knew there was something familiar; then it came to me, and I dug up this damned thing! I tell you, it tallies so close I'm damned near tempted to pull you in and send a wire to New Mexico, in spite of Selden vouching for it that you aren't the man."

Bannister drew a breath, as he laid the poster on the desk. "I could hardly blame you," he said. "So it's lucky all around that you're too smart a man to make that kind of mistake, or seem to question the word of someone as important as Boyd Selden. After all, there's no reason in the world—is there?—why he'd want to protect a man his own company is this anxious to hang."

Sourly, Tom Slate shook his head. "Not a single damn reason!"

"Then, there you have it," Jim Bannister said. And nodding good night he left the lawman staring at the poster, in bafflement. He stepped out into the crisp night, and gently closed the office door behind him.

Boyd Selden and the miner, Jud Murrow, were earnestly talking. As Bannister approached he heard the miner saying, "All right, Mister Selden, What you had to offer always did sound like a fair deal to me; but I've given my word and I have to do what the others say. By morning, when it's had a chance to sink in how Lewt Flagg was using them—they just may be willing to listen to you."

"I'll talk to anybody—anytime," Selden said.

They shook hands and Bannister watched the miner walk away. He moved up beside the syndicate man.

He said, "You going to make a deal with those Turkey Ridge men, after all?"

"I rather think so," the other told him. "Murrow can't be the only one who's begun to realize it takes capital, and not muscle alone, to work a silver claim. And now you've changed everything, the way you blew the lid off the situation in this camp!" he added, in a tone of real respect. "I swear I don't know yet how you managed—or how you got out alive!"

Bannister shrugged aside the compliment. He was not forgetting his last angry conversation with Boyd Selden. He said now, stiffly, "That still leaves J. T. Herron as the stumbling block to your company taking over the whole ridge."

"I'm not so sure of that." Window light, falling upon them, showed him the faint smile that quirked the other's lips. "Unless I'm mistaken, Herron's in his office this evening. The bank is just around the corner from here; I think we'd better drop by and see him."

He started walking in that direction; Bannister, stiff with all the punishment his body had taken, fell in step. "What business have you got that can't wait till morning?"

"Why, if I waited an hour, it could be too late!"

"I don't understand," Bannister said. But

199

then he did, suddenly, and he swore beneath his breath. "By God, I'm finally learning! You intend to close a deal while Herron still thinks the Teakettle is worthless—before he's had a chance to find out how Miles Kimrey was lying to him! You can call that smart business if you want to; but you pull it off, and it will make you just as big a crook as Kimrey ever was!"

They had reached the corner by the bank; light from a carbide streetlamp fell full upon them as Boyd Selden swung around, stung by the other's words. His face looking oddly mottled; his eyes narrowed as he suggested, "Feeling that way about it, perhaps you have some notion of tipping Herron off, yourself!"

"I never said—" Bannister began hotly, but a sudden change in Selden's face and in the direction of his stare caused him to break off and turn, for a look at what might be happening at the bank's Main Street entrance.

A small crowd of men had gathered in front of the Herron Building and more were swelling it, a cluster that overflowed the sidewalk and spilled into the street. They stood, waiting and expectant, focusing on the door with its fake Grecian pillars. Quickly, quarrel forgotten, Boyd Selden muttered an exclamation and headed that way, the other man following more slowly.

He watched Selden tap someone on the shoulder and ask a question. In the growing hum of excitement Bannister caught no more than a word: "Shot . . ." Suddenly the voices swelled, and Bannister saw a clot of men were coming down the steps and into the street.

One was bareheaded, dazed in appearance, his clothing rumpled and a smear of blood on his face where someone must have hit him. Two others gripped him firmly by wrists and elbows; yelling for the crowd to give way, they marched their prisoner between them, unresisting, out onto the sidewalk and started him in the direction of the jail. They ignored the questions that were babbled at them.

Boyd Selden was already shoving impatiently through to the door and, with Bannister close behind, climbed the double flight of stairs. No one interfered. At the top floor a door stood open, light flooding out of it. They went through the small outer chamber and into the extravagantly furnished office of J. T. Herron.

The old bookkeeper, still wearing eyeshade and black sleeve protectors, hovered in the background—pale as the map on the wall behind him, futilely wringing his hands. Behind the big desk sat J. T. Herron, where he had been flung hard against the base of his chair by the bullet that turned his silk shirt and wide cravat and waistcoat into a mass of blood. He was dead. His head had fallen to one side; the eyes were crescents of white beneath drooping lids, his jaw hung slackly open. On her knees, clutching him, Flora Gentry leaned her head against his arm and wept brokenly, heedless of the blood that smeared her hands and clothing.

Aghast, Jim Bannister looked at the clerk. "What happened?"

The man flapped his hands as he tried for speech. "He simply walked in—never said a word. I—I tried to keep him out, but the gun in his hand—"

"Who was it?" Boyd Selden demanded. "He must have had a motive. . . ."

The Gentry woman lifted her head then; from the look of her eyes she probably didn't even register their faces clearly. "It was my husband," she said, her voice dull with shock. "We gave him money—all he ever asked for. We thought he'd gone clear out of our lives, to California or maybe Australia. But I guess all these months he must have been brooding and jealous—killing jealous!" A shudder racked her. "I *knew*—I knew from the dreams, something was going to happen! God knows I tried to prevent it. But I never thought of—*this!*" She dropped her face into her hands. Her shoulders shook with weeping.

"She wanted Herron to have a bodyguard," Bannister said slowly. "She'd have hired me, but I turned her down. She was convinced someone would try to kill him, only she thought it would be some business rival. And Herron wouldn't listen . . ."

They had walked as far as the hotel in silence, stunned by the irony of what they had witnessed, speaking only now as they halted before the dark veranda. Jim Bannister added, "What do you suppose will become of her?"

"Who knows?" the syndicate man said gruffly. "Let's just hope she has some cash, or that her clothes and jewelry are worth something. Because anything Herron may have left, she won't have a claim to it. He still has a wife, somewhere in Kansas—Topeka, I think."

"So I heard."

"Along with everything else, that woman will get all his mining properties—including the Teakettle mine. Perhaps I'm just as pleased," he added, in a tone that made Bannister look at him.

"Why?"

Boyd Selden lifted a hand and dropped it. He said gruffly, "Because now I won't have to bother my conscience trying to steal the damn thing! You're pretty rough on a man, Jim Bannister—I hope you realize that! It's hard enough doing my job, without someone constantly scolding at my ethics! Perhaps you think I like some of the deals I have to make? Well, I'll let the company send somebody else to deal with Herron's widow," he went on, not giving the other time for a reply.

203

"Right now I'm chiefly interested in some sleep. I'll see you in the morning."

"No," Bannister said, and something in his tone halted the man as he was about to turn away. "You won't be seeing me. I'm pulling out—now. I've got my horse waiting; and it really doesn't look as though you'll be needing me here any longer."

It was a moment before Selden answered. "What about the statement that Tom Slate wants?"

"He'll have Jud Murrow's; that should be enough. I figure it's better if he doesn't lay eyes on me again."

"I see." Selden understood. "He's threatened you with that damned poster!" The syndicate man swore feelingly. "I thought I had convinced him."

"Twelve thousand is hard to convince—and besides, that *is* a good drawing of me. If he stares at it long enough, sooner or later he's bound to make up his mind to haul me in. I won't wait for that."

Selden nodded. "You've already been put through more here than either of us reckoned on." He thrust out a hand then. "All right—I'll cover for you with Slate. Good luck, Bannister. You've earned it!"

The other took the hand, but he suggested, "Aren't you forgetting something?"

Selden looked at him. "What?" he demanded cautiously.

"You hired me for a hundred dollars a day. You owe me two hundred."

"I'll be damned! Well, I guess you earned that, too." The syndicate man took out his billfold, counted out the amount in greenbacks and handed it over. He said, "We'll keep in touch, through the people in Morgantown. God willing, perhaps I'll have something helpful yet to pass on to you."

"Perhaps." As he pocketed the money Bannister couldn't help adding, "It's been an interesting two days. You've taught me a few things I didn't know about big business. I'm sorry I was a difficult pupil."

Boyd Selden swore at him, without heat. "You're learning, Bannister—you're learning!"

Bannister watched the other mount the steps and enter the hotel; afterward, moving stiffly, he headed for the place where he had left the dun—body crying for rest, yet anxious to put this camp behind him and to be alone again with the clean dark, under the wide stars where a man on the dodge could still find moments of freedom, and of peace.

Books are produced in the United States using U.S.-based materials

Books are printed using a revolutionary new process called THINKtech™ that lowers energy usage by 70% and increases overall quality

Books are durable and flexible because of Smyth-sewing

Paper is sourced using environmentally responsible foresting methods and the paper is acid-free

Center Point Large Print
600 Brooks Road / PO Box 1
Thorndike, ME 04986-0001 USA

(207) 568-3717

US & Canada:
1 800 929-9108
www.centerpointlargeprint.com